Holly Jolly *Heresy*

An *Aster Bay* Novella

CARA DION

Print ISBN: 979-8-9986457-2-3
Ebook ISBN: 979-8998645716

Imprint: Independently published
First edition

Cover illustration by Elen Bushe.
Cover design by Brenna Jones Design.

Also by Cara Dion

Aster Bay series:

Whisking It All
Just For Show
First Comes Marriage
Claim to Fame
Holly Jolly Heresy

Love Song series:

Irreplaceable
Indiscreet
Undeniable

**Visit my website to learn more
and download free bonus content:**

Content Warning

This book contains discussions of religion (specifically Catholicism), including how it relates to women's reproductive rights and homophobia (brief mentions).

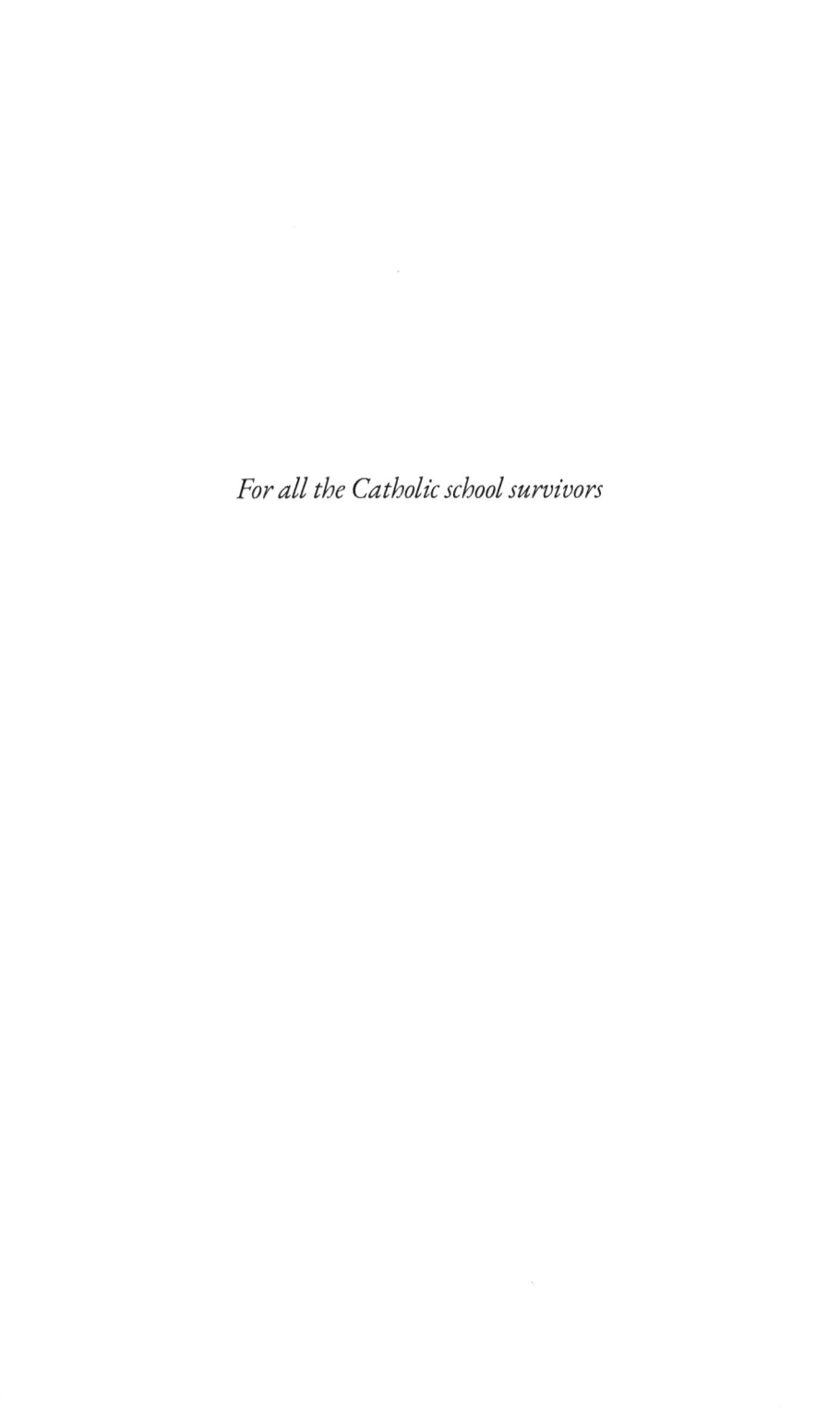

For all the Catholic school survivors

Chapter One

December 21st

I t is a truth universally acknowledged that high school teachers are in need of a good hiding place the day before Christmas break. Even if that Christmas break might be their last.

For Caleb West, there was no better hiding place than the confessional booth in St. Anthony High School's chapel. The final Mass of the term had ended hours before and even the most faithful students in the small Rhode Island school had long since abandoned the space. In a few hours, the halls of the school would be empty, too, as students, bundled against the harsh New England wind, left for two weeks of break.

But Caleb couldn't wait a few hours to read the email waiting for him on his laptop. The notification had startled him as he'd finished lecturing in his last sophomore religion class for the term. He'd been unable to stop thinking about it ever since, his hands shaking as he'd methodically erased the whiteboard and closed down his classroom for the term.

True, he could have read the message on his phone, but this wasn't a phone email. This was a big screen email. An email that required time to read properly, carefully, and the space to let the words rattle around in his brain uninterrupted.

Caleb moved through the aisles hung with swags of itchy fake greenery and slipped into the priest's side of the confessional booth. He closed the door softly behind him, gripped his laptop tightly in his free hand, and sat on the hard bench. The familiar smell of old wood and incense did little to calm his racing pulse.

Dear Father West,

I understand the predicament you face. Indeed, many priests at one time or another question their vocation. I have attached the paperwork you requested, but I once again urge you to consider a transfer to a different parish rather than pursuing laicization. A new assignment could allow for a fresh start, away from this crisis of conscience, as you've called it. Surely the inconvenience of relocating is worth the spiritual guidance you could provide a new community.

I urge you to seek counsel from your confessor, and we can discuss the matter further after Christmas...

Caleb slammed his laptop closed and let his head drop back against the wooden wall behind him. He should have known it wouldn't be that easy—not that leaving the priesthood would be *easy*, but he wasn't sure staying was possible either. A new parish could be the answer, far from his friends and family, far from his hometown of Aster Bay.

Far from *her*.

Molly Proulx.

The prettiest temptation he'd ever run across in his twenty-five years as a priest. The one temptation he wasn't sure he could resist for much longer.

But maybe this was a sign. As it was, he'd struggled to even type out the request to the Diocese. He'd been in counseling with the Bishop and his confessor for months now, but that hadn't made it any easier to admit he didn't just want a new assignment—he wanted a new life. But maybe the Bishop had a point. Besides, what would he even do if he wasn't a priest?

He scrubbed his hand over his face, breathing out the guilt twining itself around his bones and breathing in the deep, rich scent of the frankincense and myrrh from the morning's Mass.

This would be an ideal time to pray, to ask God for guidance, for strength to forget about the high school English teacher invading his every thought—but no words came. Just as no words had come to him for weeks now.

Because you don't want to pray. You don't want to remove the temptation from your thoughts.

Reassignment would be the easiest solution. He'd go somewhere far away and forget all about Molly Proulx and the maddening way she challenged him and her whiskey-colored eyes. Maybe then he wouldn't be questioning everything he thought he knew about the Church, about himself. Maybe then the doubts that kept him awake well past midnight each night would finally let him be.

From the other side of the confessional booth, a creak cut through Caleb's existential crisis as the door opened and someone slid inside. The door closed behind them with a soft snick. He held his breath as Molly's soft sigh filled the space, the spicy citrus scent curling under his nose as though he'd summoned her with his thoughts. *Cinnamon and bergamot.*

Shuffling on the other side, his view obscured by the screen between their booths, and then the click of Tupperware opening, the unmistakable crunch of chewing. Caleb pressed his lips together, suppressing a smile. Perhaps he wasn't the only one who had discovered the virtues of hiding in a confessional.

"Ms. Proulx?" he asked softly.

She yelped in surprise, the sharp sound followed by a muttered curse and more shuffling. "Father West? What are you doing here?"

"Are you really asking what a priest is doing in a confessional?" He grinned despite himself.

"Shit—I mean, sorry, Father, are you...holding office hours or something?"

"Office hours?" he snorted.

"Or whatever it's called when you hang out in there and wait for people to come tell you their sins."

"It's called confession."

"I didn't mean to interrupt. I was looking for a place to eat where Mr. Day couldn't commandeer my lunch break."

More shuffling, as though she was gathering her things to leave. But Caleb couldn't very well send her back out there to contend with the overzealous principal. She should be able to eat her salad in peace.

"You're not interrupting. Stay."

"You're sure?"

"I'm sure."

A few moments of silence, the muffled sounds of her eating. Then, "This is weird."

"Why?"

"Because I can't see you. You're just...listening to me eat?"

Caleb slid back the screen separating their booths, revealing the woman on the other side. Molly wore a white turtleneck sweater, the knit material hugging her ample curves and wrapping around her throat, her chestnut hair loose around her shoulders. His gaze lingered on her mouth, the sheen of oil on her lips from her salad dressing as she ate.

It took some effort for him to look away. "Better?"

"Better." She settled against the side of the confessional, turning her body towards him as she poked around in the plastic container before spearing a cherry tomato and popping the red orb into her mouth. "So, Father, if you're not hearing confessions, what are you doing?"

"I am also hiding from Mr. Day."

She laughed, the sound bouncing off the wood so foreign in this space it made him laugh as well. "I know why he's after me, but why's he after you?"

Caleb sighed. It was no secret that he and the principal of St. Anthony High butted heads regularly. Bruce Day was a "letter of the law" kind of guy, and Caleb...wasn't. Especially when it came to caring for the students. And while Caleb might be the spiritual leader of the school, Bruce was the disciplinarian, a role he seemed bound and determined to wield like his very own fiery sword, leading the teenagers in their care to the path of righteousness through fear and punishment if necessary. Caleb was more of a "the greatest of these is love" kind of leader, something Bruce saw as eminently distasteful and untrustworthy. Mostly Caleb just stayed out of Bruce's way.

"He's decided he needs to balance the secularity of our drama department by adding more religious pageants into the school calendar." Caleb could barely keep the disdain from his voice.

"More pageants? Do we do *any* pageants right now?"

"None. Which is apparently the problem. He was not satisfied by my answer that the students at St. Catherine's Elementary do enough pageants for both schools."

Another laugh, this one tinkling and light, tinged with their shared annoyance over the principal's fanaticism. It felt like a victory, that laugh.

"Wouldn't that fall under religious education?" she asked.

"If only. Then I could overrule him. He's decided it's an extracurricular club, and when I tried to argue against it for budgetary reasons, he countered that he's already secured all the costumes we could ever need from a Catholic school in Maine that closed down at the end of last year. I'm heading there tomorrow to pick them up."

"He's not going himself?"

Caleb shot her a wry look. "That's exactly why I'm hiding. After he badgered me until I agreed to make the trip, he added that he'd be happy to go with me. Apparently, the pastor in Maine said we'd need at least two people to pack everything up. Bruce called it a pilgrimage."

"The two of you trapped together in a car for that long? One of you isn't coming back alive."

"Don't I know it. If someone else wanted to come, I could get him to stand down."

She hummed thoughtfully as she speared another tomato.

"I was going to ask Hannah to go since she knows about costumes, and honestly the theater department will probably end up stuck leading these pageants eventually anyway, but I don't know her well yet..."

"I'll go."

Caleb's heart stopped, every muscle in his body tensing. "You want to go to Maine with me?"

She shrugged, her eyes trained on her salad as she turned over the lettuce with her fork, digging for croutons and cucumbers. "Sure. Jo's using our apartment for a photo shoot tomorrow so I can't stay home. And I've been helping Hannah with costumes since last year, so maybe I could be helpful. It beats hiding out at a coffee shop all day."

His palms itched and the back of his neck tingled with awareness. *Lead us not into temptation...* "It'll be a long day. Three and a half hours each way."

"I don't mind." She glanced up at him, her brows drawn together and uncertainty flashing in her eyes. "Unless you don't want me to come. I didn't mean to—"

"No, of course, I'd love for you to come." He swallowed hard, his pulse racing and heat washing over him. "Great idea." *It's a terrible idea.*

She smiled as though she only half believed him. "Can I be the one to tell Bruce?"

"If you really want to."

"That zealot is making me swap *Macbeth* for *Romeo and Juliet* because he doesn't like the 'unsex me' scene. Between that and the way he's been treating Alex..." She cut herself off, pressing her lips together, and snapped the lid on her

Tupperware before sliding it back into the padded lunch bag at her feet.

Caleb wanted to ask what she meant about Alex. The quiet senior mostly kept to himself, and Caleb couldn't imagine a scenario that would have put the honor roll student at odds with the principal.

"This is the only chance I'm going to have to take something away from Bruce," Molly said.

"You're a petty, evil genius."

Molly dipped her head in acknowledgment, her lips curling up in a grin that matched his own.

They stared at each other for a moment through the opening between the booths, grinning like fools, and Caleb's heart thudded painfully in his chest, straining against his ribcage.

The shrill ring of the school bell sounded, signaling the end of the lunch period and pulling him back to reality.

"I better get back to my classroom." Molly reached for her lunch bag. "Tomorrow?"

"Tomorrow. Meet me at the church at nine?"

"See you then." She got to her feet and paused with her hand on the door to the confessional, almost as though she had something else to say, but thought better of it. Instead, she dipped her head again, her soft smile turning almost sad. "Father West."

His own smile fell, and when he said her name, it was more like a prayer than any words he'd said in weeks. "Ms. Proulx."

Chapter Two

December 22nd

"Would you rather never eat pizza again, or only eat pizza for the rest of your life?" Molly asked, tossing another gummy bear from the bag in the cupholder into her mouth.

"Easy. Never eat pizza again," Caleb said.

"Seriously? You know your answer that fast?"

"There are so many foods in the world. You'd trade them all for pizza?" He glanced at her as he steered the car into the center travel lane of the highway and adjusted the cruise control. They'd been driving for a little over an hour and a half and traffic was moving slowly, but at least it was moving. And if a few extra cars on the road meant Molly got a few extra minutes with Caleb, well, she didn't exactly mind.

"There are so many different kinds of pizza, though. You've got your classics—pepperoni, eggplant, margherita—"

"I'm familiar." He smirked, the corner of his mouth kicking up in a way that should not have been adorable but was completely irresistible all the same.

Get it together, Molly. He's a priest for Christ's sake.

"And then you have your breakfast pizzas."

"Is that like a breakfast burrito?"

"Similar concept. Fewer beans."

He chuckled, the sound low and rich, like molasses.

"And you can't forget dessert pizzas."

"Dessert pizzas," he repeated as though he thought he had misheard her.

"The Pizza Stone makes one with Nutella, sliced strawberries, and whipped cream. It's incredible."

"That's not pizza."

"Anything's pizza if you put it on a pizza crust."

"And for a Nutella-pizza-crust monstrosity, you'd give up pasta? Ice cream? Fresh sourdough bread?"

Molly scoffed and dug into the gummy bear bag again in search of an elusive clear gummy. "No, definitely not."

"But you said—"

"I just wanted to be sure you'd given my question the consideration it was due."

He laughed and held out his hand, indicating the candy in her hand with a waggle of his eyebrow. "Bear me."

She lifted a handful of gummy bears from the bag and dropped them into his open palm. He deposited the entire handful in his mouth in a move more appropriate for their students than for a forty-six-year-old priest.

"Your turn," she said.

"Hmmm... Eggnog or hot chocolate?"

She scoffed. "Hot chocolate. Next."

"I'm not sure you gave my question the consideration it was due," he teased.

"There's nothing to consider. Eggnog is gross and hot chocolate is delightful."

"Valid."

Molly turned slightly towards Caleb. The sun gilded his profile, accentuating the strong slope of his nose, the square cut of his jaw...and the white collar peeking out at the top of his shirt. It wasn't that she ever forgot Caleb was a priest, but somehow, over the last year since he'd taken over at St. Anthony's, she'd come to see him as so much more. She'd always thought priests were stuffy old men with severe expressions ranting about fire and brimstone, not a silver fox-in-training with a smile that lit up his whole face and a way of speaking that made her feel like the only person in the room. Not this man with his hazel and gold eyes that crinkled at the corners when he smiled and biceps that strained the fabric of his shirts, muscled forearms that were far too distracting when he wore short sleeves, hands so large and warm it was impossible not to imagine how they'd feel on her skin—

Still a priest. Still very much off limits and entirely inappropriate to fantasize about.

Though there had been that one night last May, when he had almost seemed to invite her to forget about his vocation and the twenty-year age difference between them.

"Did you always want to be a priest?" His eyebrows lifted and she winced. "Sorry. Is that rude to ask?"

"No. I wasn't expecting the question, that's all."

"I just realized I've never asked you and... You joined the priesthood really young, didn't you? I remember Gavin saying something about that."

His smile seemed more rueful than pleased. "My baby brother does love telling the story of my calling."

"Is that what it was? A calling?"

He hesitated and again she got the sense she'd stumbled into a question he didn't want her to ask. "I thought it was. At the time." She let the words settle between them, waiting for him to continue. "No, I didn't always want to be a priest. But, to be fair, I didn't want to be anything."

"You didn't dream of being a firefighter when you were a kid? I thought little boys always wanted to be firefighters."

"Maybe when I was little, but by the time I was old enough people were asking me that question, I didn't have an answer."

He glanced at her, as though he was weighing how much to say, his eyes swimming with his unspoken thoughts. When he turned back to the road, a smile slid over his lips that looked nothing like the smiles he usually gave her. This was his politicking smile, the one he reserved for parents' night and meetings with Bruce. That smile sank in her stomach like a lead weight.

"What about you?" he asked. "Did you always know you wanted to be a teacher?"

Molly turned away, focusing on the trees whipping by on the side of the highway through her window. "No. I became an English major because I wanted to read all day. But right before my junior year, my parents reminded me that eventually I'd need to be able to pay my bills, and no one was going to hire me to read. They suggested I become a librarian, but Williston didn't have a library sciences degree. I think they were hoping I'd move home, but I enrolled in the education school instead."

"You're telling me if Williston University had a library degree, we wouldn't even be sitting here right now?"

She shrugged. "We might be. Your brother *did* marry one of my best friends."

"But you're such a great teacher," he spluttered.

She barked out a laugh. "How would you know? You haven't taken one of my classes."

"I know. Anyone who can get high school juniors excited about Shakespeare is a great teacher. Those kids adore you."

Her heart warmed with the compliment, but she waved it away. "I bribe them with donuts on test days."

"And you make learning fun. Having them rewrite *Othello* as a reality TV show and film the episodes? Brilliant."

Now she was blushing in earnest. She was proud of that unit, and the kids did seem to enjoy it. "I like teaching. It's not where I intended to end up, but it's been a pretty great place to land."

Tell him now.

She'd offered to come on this trip in no small part because she was hoping she'd finally find a way to tell Caleb about the job offer sitting in her email inbox that she'd been ignoring for the last week. The one that would take her away from Aster Bay. The one expecting an answer by the first of the year.

She knew what she *should* do, but every time she tried to sign the contract she thought about all the things she'd miss—the family dinners at Lemon and Thyme with their friends and the late night girl talk over too much pizza and wine while Jo recounted her latest escapades.

And Caleb.

"How did you end up teaching at St. Anthony's?"

She sighed, shooting him an unimpressed look. "This is starting to sound like a job interview."

He grinned, a real grin that lit up his whole face and made her feel like a bottle of shaken champagne. What she wouldn't give to only ever see this kind of smile from him.

"Maybe it is."

"Oh yeah? What position am I interviewing for?"

He hummed in thought, his gaze skimming over her, raising goosebumps along her arms. "Official road trip companion."

"You are asking all the wrong questions then." She reached back into the bag of gummy bears and dropped a few in his outstretched palm before plucking a bright red one for herself.

"What should I be asking?"

She chewed the gummy bear slowly before answering. "Best highway rest stop snack?"

"Easy. A giant soft pretzel. The kind with the big chunks of salt that fall off and get everywhere."

"Is there any other kind?"

"Yeah. The wrong kind."

She laughed and pointed at the sign ahead of them. "Great, then you won't mind stopping at that rest stop to grab one."

He glared at her but there was no heat in it, his lips curled in a way that made her warm all over. "You're going to make us late."

"You in a rush?"

"Not in the slightest."

Chapter Three

Nativity, Maine was a small coastal town not far from Portland. A blip of a town, really. A blink while driving down I-95 and you'll miss it kind of town. But that hadn't stopped Nativity from taking full advantage of its name and going all in on Christmas.

Snow had begun to fall as Caleb navigated the narrow streets. Fanciful designs in Christmas lights were strung overhead between the tall evergreen, maple, and oak trees lining the sidewalk, lampposts were wrapped in festive garlands, and wreaths hung on nearly every door.

He wanted to love it.

Christmas had always been Caleb's favorite holiday, but this year, he was dreading the upcoming Masses he would need to lead. How was he meant to stand in front of all those people who had known him since he was a child, who looked to him for spiritual guidance, when he had never felt so disconnected from the Church? How could he face it when, until that email the day before, he'd been certain this would be his last Christmas Mass?

"Is that—" Molly broke off, pointing ahead to the little patch of grass at the corner of the intersection where giant cow statues had been draped in fabric and arranged in a manger scene, a baby calf swaddled in the cradle.

"I think so," Caleb said. "Bruce said this town is known for its Christmas spirit."

"Is it Christmas spirit if it's moderately disturbing?"

Caleb bit back a grin, allowing his more conflicted thoughts to drift away on the tide of Molly's cynicism. "Are you not a fan of Christmas?"

"Who doesn't love Christmas? I'm not a fan of whatever that is," she said, pointing again.

On top of a fish market, another manger scene had been erected consisting entirely of giant inflatable lobsters wearing Santa hats. This time, Caleb couldn't contain his laughter, the sound flowing through him. "I think Nativity may be taking their namesake a little too literally."

"You think? Lobster baby Jesus was wearing a Santa hat. The lobster wisemen were carrying tubs of butter."

He glanced in the rearview mirror to catch another glimpse of the display. "They were not."

"Oh, they absolutely were. Is it sacrilege to imply the wisemen are going to eat baby Jesus?"

"Well, it's certainly not approved doctrine."

"Do you think it's like this all year, or only at Christmas?"

"With a name like Nativity, who knows." Caleb tilted his chin towards a toy shop proudly proclaiming itself as the North Pole South. "But I'm inclined to think this is a year-round obsession."

"It probably bodes well for the costumes. A town this invested in their nativity scenes likely didn't skimp on the Christmas pageant."

Up ahead, a rail car stood in a half-empty parking lot, the exterior strung with colorful blinking Christmas lights, a beacon shining through the beginnings of a passing flurry. A giant Christmas tree was strapped to the roof beneath an elevated, illuminated sign reading 'Railway Diner.'

"Are you hungry?" he asked.

"I could eat. Do we have time?"

"We're not meeting Father David for another hour. We have time."

Caleb pulled his coat tightly around himself as he climbed out of the car, but snowflakes slid down his open collar and stung his neck anyway. Molly didn't seem to mind the snow, however. She tilted her face up to the sky and caught a snowflake on her tongue, the tip of her nose already turning pink in the chill air. His gaze lingered on the long line of her throat, the snowflakes falling in her hair and glistening as though she'd been sprinkled with glitter. He wanted to press his nose to her hair, breathe in her scent and feel her laughter vibrate through him.

He spun away, clearing his throat, and led her up the metal steps to the door of the rail car. No good could come from indulging those fantasies.

Inside, the diner was cramped, made more so by the track suspended from the ceiling, a bright red toy train with Santa in the front car making a constant, slow circuit around the space. Where train seats had originally been on each side of the narrow aisle, booths had been installed, each one aligned with one of the rounded windows overlooking the parking lot, bundles of silver balloons tied to the coat hooks at the end of each booth. At the back of the car, a modest, open kitchen stood behind a half wall, the top of which was strung with garland and more of those blinking Christmas lights. From some unseen speaker, Burl Ives' rich baritone sang holiday classics extolling the virtues of snow and reindeer.

A petite woman with graying hair piled in a messy bun held together by multiple pens stood at the other end of the car, her arms loaded down with plates of steaming food. She tilted her chin in their direction and gestured towards one of the open booths with a bowl of soup, broth sloshing dangerously close to the edge of the bowl. "Afternoon, folks. Make yourselves at home. I'll be with you in a minute."

They chose a booth not far from the door, Caleb shrugging out of his jacket and Molly unwinding her scarf as they took their seats. "If I'd known it was going to snow, I would have worn a thicker coat," he said.

Molly's eyes lingered on his frame as he hung their things on the hook beside their table. His shoulders and biceps tingled with awareness as her gaze swept over him. The last time she'd looked at him like that...

Her voice was soft when she spoke. "I have to confess something."

He held up his hands. "Uh uh, I'm off duty."

"You're wearing your collar," she pointed out.

"I'm pretty much always wearing the collar."

"Don't worry. It's not that type of confession. I'm not really a Catholic anyway."

"You're not?" he asked, unable to hide his surprise.

"I mean, I made my First Communion, but I haven't considered myself a practicing Catholic in years. Don't tell Bruce. He'd fire me so fast."

Something irrational and wild thrummed through Caleb's blood. "I wouldn't let him."

Were her cheeks pink from the cold, or was she blushing? Caleb wasn't sure, but he knew he was far too fascinated by the changes in her skin tone for his own good.

"What's your confession?" he asked.

She lowered her voice. "I kind of want to make my own ridiculous nativity scene now."

He couldn't help the surprised laugh bubbling up from his throat. "Yeah? What would you use for yours?"

"Hmm. I bet I could get Tessa to make nativity scene themed cupcakes, like those Barbie cakes with the doll in the middle."

"Can't say I'm familiar."

"Well, then you are missing out, my friend."

"What flavor would these cupcakes be?"

She tsked. "You really aren't familiar. It's not about the cake. It's all about the frosting. Gobs of it piped to look like ruffled dresses and with way too much food coloring mixed in."

"Are you planning to put baby Jesus in a ruffled frosting dress?"

"No worse than a Santa hat and a tin of butter."

"Fair point."

The waitress arrived at their table, plucking a pen from her bun and a small notepad from her apron. "Can I get you folks something to drink? Coffee? Tea?"

"Water will be fine, thanks," Molly said.

Caleb nodded in agreement as the waitress handed them each an oversized laminated menu.

"Today's special is gingerbread pancakes with candied orange peel and powdered sugar. Oh, and a tuna melt with Swiss on rye. I'll give you a minute to look over the menu." And then she was gone again.

"It's like I've stumbled into a made-for-TV Christmas movie," Caleb said as he perused the menu.

"Nope. If this were a Christmas movie, I would be a big city lawyer and you would be the sweet and humble, inexplicably unmarried bachelor who runs a Christmas tree farm and teaches me to believe in magic after an hour of cheesy run-ins and exactly one kiss." Her eyes flickered down to his lips and then darted away again.

Caleb's pulse jumped, and he forced himself to focus on the menu instead of the images running through his head at the mere idea of kissing Molly, of how his hands were fit on her waist, the way his fingers would sink into her hips when he pulled her closer—

This had been a bad idea. He should have made the trip himself, or let Bruce come with him. Why did he think spending the entire day with Molly would do anything but make him even more unreasonably drawn to her?

You didn't. You knew that's what would happen. And you did it anyway.

"Have we decided?" the waitress asked, reappearing at their table.

"Turkey club." He handed the menu back, even though he'd barely looked at it. Surely a diner had a turkey club on the menu.

"Banana pancakes," Molly said.

"Did you want whipped cream and powdered sugar?" the waitress asked.

"Just butter and syrup, thanks."

"Suit yourself, honey."

When the waitress was safely out of earshot, Molly leaned across the table, lowering her voice. "Do you think they put powdered sugar on everything here? You better watch out. Your turkey club might come with a dusting of sugar."

Her whiskey eyes were so beautiful they made all his other thoughts drift away. And when she teased him like that, like they were any two people and not a priest and his sister-in-law's friend...

With that sparkle in Molly's eyes and the way it made him want to reach across the table—*this* was why he should let himself be reassigned. Now. Yesterday. Before he did something he couldn't take back.

Her eyes narrowed slightly, as though she could hear his thoughts. Or maybe he'd just been staring.

"Molly—

She tilted her chin towards the bundle of silver balloons tied to the end of their booth. "Do you ever think about that night last May?"

His mouth went dry and his lungs burned, but he couldn't tear his gaze away from her. Unsure what to do with the restless feeling suddenly coursing through him, he clasped his hands between his thighs.

Last May, Caleb and Molly had found themselves alone after hours at school, decorating the hallway for the tradition of the senior entrance. Tangled in blue and white crepe paper streamers, an ocean of silver balloons at their feet, they'd talked long after the last poster was hung, laughed until they were both drunk with it. It was the only explanation for the way their bodies had gravitated towards each other, for the temporary insanity of turning his face into her hair, the cinnamon and bergamot scent of her so revelatory he still imagined he could smell it late at night when his thoughts drifted to things he could never admit. Their goodbye hug had lingered a little too long, hands skating over backs and waists with a little too much reluctance to withdraw, and she'd looked at him with those big eyes like she could see every part of him.

That night, he'd almost broken his vows mere steps from his own chapel.

"I think about that night a lot," she continued. "I liked seeing that side of you."

He forced himself to swallow, bringing moisture back to his mouth, and folded his hands on the table. "What side?"

"You were...different. Relaxed. Sometimes it feels like you're performing or something, like you're always aware of people watching you."

"Because they are."

She nodded. "But not that night. You were just...Caleb." His throat constricted around the words he wouldn't allow himself to say as a sad sort of smile tilted up her lips. "I liked it."

"I liked it too."

"I even liked your dance moves." He barked out a laugh, her sudden teasing releasing the tension building in his chest, and her smile widened. "Very Hugh Grant in *Love Actually*."

"Ouch." He clapped a hand over his heart. "I think I should be offended."

"You have some impressive hip action."

"It's all that ballroom dancing in Mrs. White's class at the senior center." He chuckled to himself. "She's determined to make me the perfect rumba partner. Right now, Gavin puts me to shame."

"You can't be outdone by your little brother."

"Never." The laughter fell away, replaced by something softer, more truthful. "I liked dancing with you."

"More than with Mrs. White?" she teased.

"Much more."

Her lips pressed together, and her eyebrows furrowed, despite her valiant effort to maintain her smile. "Why did you become a priest, Caleb?"

He hesitated, the practiced story of his calling springing to his lips as it had so many times over the last twenty-five years. A story he'd told so often he almost believed it himself.

But that wasn't the story he wanted to tell her. He wanted her to know the other story—the one he'd only ever told his confessor.

"After my dad died, when I was little, Mom started taking us to church a lot more. She said Dad was with God and we could tell Him what we wanted Dad to know—the baseball games we won or the first time I jumped off the diving board without holding my nose. And I never understood. Why did I have to talk to an intermediary? Why couldn't I just talk to my dad?"

She leaned forward, her fingers inching closer to him across the linoleum tabletop but stopping short of actually making contact with his skin.

"For a while, I stopped going, and I know it broke Mom's heart. She was so comforted by the Church, and I was just...angry. I was so angry for so long I think I stopped even registering it as an emotion. It was just my state of being. But even through all the anger, I kept praying, hoping someone would talk back someday—God, or my Dad, it didn't even matter because by that point they were so intertwined in my head."

"I told my mom God talked to me one day when I was around seven or eight," Molly said, her fingers mere millimeters from where his hands rested on the table.

"What did He say?"

"To get off his lawn."

Caleb laughed, loud and deep, and her lips turned up at the corners in response, though her eyes remained soft, focused on him, as though she knew he needed a reprieve from telling his story.

"Of course, I didn't tell her until later that I was talking to the old man who lived next door. He had a long white beard, and his name was Mr. Lord."

"You thought God was your neighbor?"

"Seemed more reasonable than an invisible, omniscient deity. My mother was unamused. She'd told all her friends I was blessed but the whole time I was just getting into shouting matches with my crotchety old neighbor over the ball I lost in his yard."

He hung his head, smiling, taking a moment to imagine seven-year-old Molly's feud with her neighbor. "I wanted to yell at God," he continued, focusing his eyes on the space between their hands. Hardly any distance at all, but one he couldn't cross. "Instead, I got in trouble. A lot of trouble."

"What kind of trouble?"

"Stupid kid stuff. I broke into the high school the night before graduation and TP'd the principal's office. Set all the frogs in the biology lab free my freshman year of college. Things like that."

"Why?"

"Because maybe I wasn't being loud enough." He met her eyes, desperate for her to understand. "I believed the stories. I believed them so much it hurt, because Moses got a burning bush and Joseph got dreams, and Paul got a voice on the road to Damascus, and I got *nothing*."

His chest heaved, the pain of those years still jagged beneath his ribs. And she waited, her gaze steady and patient, as her pinky dragged along the edge of his hand. Just once. A single swipe of her skin on his, a balm and torture all at once.

"Then one day, just before Christmas break my freshman year of college, I went to the chapel on campus. To this day, I'm not sure what I intended to do, but I was angrier than I'd ever been and I wanted to know He saw. That He knew. I wanted Him to take some responsibility for the tangled-up mess He'd made of me."

"What happened?"

"I met Father Raymond. And it felt like, for the first time, God was listening." He pulled his hands away, dropping them in his lap, though each fraction of an inch he put between them felt wrong. "He helped me find a way through the mess and the anger, and when I didn't know what to do with my time if I wasn't being mad at God anymore, Father Raymond told me I should try loving Him instead."

"How?"

"By loving His people. By helping other angry, mixed-up kids know they are loved. Father Raymond showed me I could have a purpose, a way to turn my years of frustration into something good. Something to help people. I contacted the Diocese the next day."

Her brow furrowed in something he would have called confusion if she didn't look so pained by it. "God isn't the one who makes angry, mixed-up kids doubt they are loved, Caleb," she said, her voice shaking slightly. "The Church does that."

He bristled at the accusation. "No institution is perfect."

"Institutions protect themselves, not the people in them," she practically spat, the frustration in her words bubbling over.

He blinked, struggling to place the source of the sudden shift in her mood, the unexpected hurt of it dragging his own frustrations to the surface. "Are you...mad at me for joining the priesthood?"

Her cheeks flushed scarlet, and she avoided making eye contact. "I'm not mad at you, Father."

He winced at her use of the honorific, the word slashing across his skin as the new, fragile closeness between them begin to crumble. Caleb swallowed down the bitterness at the loss. Distance was safer anyway.

"Here we are!" The waitress reappeared, her arms loaded down with their lunch, but all Caleb could see was Molly, her whiskey eyes and the freckles across the bridge of her nose that he'd memorized months ago and the disappointed downturn of her lips.

Molly, who saw him in ways he hadn't been seen in so long he'd almost forgotten what it was like to have someone see *him* before they saw his profession.

Molly, who challenged him as he hadn't been challenged in decades, who tangled him up inside in new, exciting ways that made him never want to unravel it.

He'd said something wrong. Somehow, he'd let her down. A clawing, scraping need dragged itself up his throat, desperate to snatch back whichever words had put that look on her face, to make her understand, to go back to easy smiles and banter about pizza.

Tell her the truth.

But what truth would make her look at him with that sparkle in her eyes again? The truth that he'd devoted the last twenty-five years of his life to an institution he was no longer sure he believed in? That everything he knew about faith, about God, was telling him one thing while the Church he'd vowed to serve told him something else entirely? That he wanted her to understand how he'd gotten here, even if he was more convinced by the day it was a mistake? That he was terrified to leave because he didn't know who he was anymore if he wasn't a priest?

Except you do. You're the man you are when you're with her.

She blinked, her eyes clearing and her smile stuttering, before it morphed into the plastic version she wore at faculty meetings. He hated it, wanted to reach across the table and drag his thumb across her bottom lip to wipe the lie from her face. He'd thought they were getting closer, but she'd never felt farther away.

She reached for her fork and knife. "This looks delicious. Do you want some?"

"Molly." His voice was hoarse.

"Thank you. For telling me. I really am grateful."

"You seem angry."

"It's okay to be angry sometimes, Caleb. Even at God, and maybe especially at the Church."

He opened his mouth to speak, but no sound came out, her words buzzing beneath his skin like a hornet's nest burst open in his veins.

She gestured to her pancakes again with her knife. "You sure you don't want any?"

"Yeah."

"Yeah?"

"I mean, no. I don't want any. Thank you."

He watched with rapt attention as she carved off a triangle of pancake and popped it into her mouth, her eyes fluttering closed as she ate. An answering jolt of electricity raced down his spine immediately followed by a nauseating wave of guilt as those hornets continued to buzz.

Something had shifted between them. Somehow he'd put more distance between them when all he wanted was to bring her closer. His muscles burned with the restraint required to keep from reaching for her hand, to stop himself from bringing them back to the moment when her finger glided against his skin and he thought he might die from the pleasure of it.

Worse still, he knew now, without a shadow of a doubt, he would do whatever it took to get her to look at him again the way she did that night last May.

Chapter Four

By the time they left the diner, a few inches of snow had accumulated on the ground, and Molly's frustration had cooled to a low simmer. The whole time they'd eaten, she'd felt Caleb's eyes on her, studying her, worry pressing his lips into a flat line. It didn't matter how she tried to steer the conversation to lighter things, the weight of those few strained exchanges remained between them.

Maybe it wasn't fair of her, to want him to recognize the failings of his Church, the innumerable ways it passively inflicted harm on the students entrusted to its care, but she couldn't help it. He was a good man—she knew he was. Was it too much to hope he'd see the morbid irony in his joining the priesthood to help the very kids the Church hurt most?

"Did you know it was going to snow today?" Molly asked, trying once again to get them back to the easy place they'd been in before she went and asked for his origin story.

"No. Did you?"

"I never check the weather forecast. It's wrong most of the time anyway."

Caleb chuckled, but it wasn't as light and free as his laughter had been earlier in the day. Her stomach twisted in knots.

"We'll get the costumes from Father David and be headed home in less than an hour. I'm sure it'll be fine," Caleb said as he steered the car back out onto the main road.

Sure, it would be fine, but would *they* be fine?

Blessed Sacrament Catholic School may have been closed for over six months, but that hadn't stopped the town of Nativity from decorating the lot at the edge of town. A massive nativity scene was spread across the snow-covered lawn, each life-size character depicted on a painted piece of plywood, the faces carefully cut out to allow passersby to take their photos as the Virgin Mary or a wiseman or even as a lamb tucked away in a pile of hay. The only figure with a face was the baby Jesus, whose painted features crossed into uncanny valley territory, especially surrounded by his faceless coterie.

"That's creepy, right? It's not just me?" Molly asked.

"Definitely not just you."

"I never considered myself a grinch, but in the face of all *this,* I'm starting to wonder."

Caleb shook his head. "Hate to break it to you, Mol, but you could never be a grinch. Your heart is too big."

His words sent confused butterflies fluttering in her stomach, butterflies that had no business occupying any part of her anatomy. She was annoyed with him, dammit, and frustrated by his tacit compliance with a system continuously hurting the very kids he claimed to be trying to help. But she was also captivated by his easy charm, intrigued by the vulnerability in his voice when he'd told her about his path to the priesthood, delighted by his soft words and lingering glances...

Butterflies were out of the question. Her feelings for Caleb were already complicated enough without adding flying insects into the equation.

Caleb parked the car and marched up the walk to greet the priest standing in the open doorway of the decommissioned school. Molly followed after him, half-jogging to keep up with his long strides.

"Father West, it's so good to see you again," the priest said, shaking Caleb's hand. "What has it been? Ten years?"

"At least. Good to see you, too, Father David. Thank you for this."

"We're happy to have the costumes go to a good home." Father David peered around Caleb's shoulder. "Is this one of your students?"

A surprised, choking sound burst from Caleb's lips as Molly appeared at his side. "Molly Proulx," she said, extending her hand towards the older man. "I'm an English teacher at St. Anthony's."

Father David's full belly laugh would have been more at home on a mall Santa. "My mistake! You'll have to excuse me, Ms. Proulx. When you get to be our age, all youth seems so out of reach, it's hard to tell how old someone is," he said, gesturing between himself and Caleb.

Molly frowned. Father David seemed significantly older than Caleb. Sure, Caleb's hair was going gray at the temples and in the scruff of his facial hair, but Father David had hardly any hair at all. Where Caleb was toned and lean, Father David was round and soft.

Caleb's horrified expression quickly morphed into one of practiced deflection. "I think you've got at least a decade on me, Father."

"Maybe, maybe. Come inside. It's freezing out here. Let's get your car loaded up and get you on your way before this snow starts falling in earnest."

They followed Father David inside a building that looked so much like St. Anthony's—the same tan brick, the same peachy-pink and off-white tile of so many Catholic schools built in the 1960s. Lagging behind the older priest, Molly leaned close to Caleb and whispered, "Just how old *are* you, Father West?"

"You know I'm forty-six," he grumbled, "and Father David is pushing sixty. At least."

Caleb may have been twenty years her senior, but she couldn't say she'd ever really noticed. Though she supposed that was probably because half her friends were coupled up with men significantly older than them—including one of her best friends, Kyla, who had married Caleb's brother, Gavin, despite their own twenty-year age difference, and the fact Kyla used to date Gavin's son.

Not that Kyla and Gavin's situation was particularly relevant to Molly and Caleb since they would never be more than colleagues. And friends. Frolleagues. Even if Caleb had starred in some of her more inconvenient, *very* dirty, decidedly non-frolleague-like thoughts.

"Here we are," Father David said, holding open the door to a classroom at the end of the long hall. The blinds were drawn, and rolling clothing racks, each heavily hung with more costumes than Molly had ever seen in one place, filled the room. There was an entire rack devoted to angel wings—sparkly ones that looked more like fairy wings and iridescent ones that reminded her of dragonflies—and another just for farm animals, though those outfits looked more like onesie pajamas than anything. Bankers' boxes and a roll of large black garbage bags sat next to the door, waiting to be filled. "Help yourself to whatever you'd like. The rest will go to the Goodwill in the morning. I'll be just down the hall if you need me."

Alone with the daunting task of packing up the costume collection, Molly and Caleb spun around, taking in the enormity of the task. "Were you expecting this much?" Molly asked.

Caleb pinched the green polyester of one of the costumes between his fingers. "I thought there'd be a few angel wings and some robes, not an entire corner dedicated to elf costumes."

"Can we please take some of these back? Just to mess with Bruce a little?" Molly asked, holding up a reindeer antler headband.

"I say we take as much of it as we can fit in the car."

The reindeer antlers were just the tip of the iceberg. Behind the rack of elf costumes ranging from demure to scandalous candy-striped fantasy, and behind the refrigerator box full of shepherd's crooks of various sizes, was an entire section of Santa costumes. There was the traditional red with oversized black buckles, of course, but also a floor length green velvet with gold tassels that looked more like the Ghost of Christmas Present, and a small section of short red velvet dresses with white faux-fur trim. Molly held one of the dresses up against herself and turned to face the floor-length mirror leaning against the back wall. The fabric ended high up on her thigh and the top would be scandalously low cut—it had clearly been made for a smaller woman—but she was intrigued nonetheless.

"I don't understand why a Catholic school has all these secular costumes. I thought the Church was against Santa," she said, smoothing the dress where it lay over her full hips.

"No one's against Santa. The Church just wants to keep the focus on—" Caleb turned from where he'd been carefully boxing angel wings, his eyes snagging on Molly. He froze, his fist tightening around the edge of one iridescent angel wing, bending the flimsy wire frame. "—Christ," he finished, the word mostly an exhale.

She shouldn't like the way his eyes darkened and his jaw clenched, the gravel sneaking into that last word as his gaze swept over her. She shouldn't be dying to know what he might say, how he might look at her, if she actually put the dress on instead of just holding it against her body.

And there are those damn butterflies again.

"I think I'm going to keep this one for myself," she said.

Caleb swallowed, his Adam's apple bobbing in his throat.

"The girls and I always go to the Christmas party at The Bay Breeze and I never have a good costume," she explained as she slid the dress off the hanger and folded it carefully. "At least not as good as Jo's."

"You should keep it then," he said, some of the roughness lingering in his tone. He cleared his throat and turned back to the angel wings, straightening the wire he'd accidentally bent while she tucked the small bundle of fabric into her purse.

"Maybe this year we'll convince you guys to come with us to the party instead of having one of your game nights at Ethan's." She grabbed a Santa hat from the top of the nearest rack and placed it on Caleb's head, eager for the distraction from the sudden heat pulsing between them.

He arched an eyebrow and pointed to the hat. "Is this my costume?"

"It's a start." She snatched the red velvet coat next and helped him into it, his amused smirk growing by the second. Her hands lingered on his chest, straightening the white fur trim as she did her best not to notice how firm his pecs were beneath her hands. Her index finger swept a gentle arc over the white clerical collar at the base of his throat, and he sucked in a breath. Instantly, she dropped her hands and stepped back.

What are you doing? You can't just touch *him. He's a priest, for God's sake.*

Molly spun back to the rack of Santa costumes. "I think we've probably got all we need from this rack. I'll go start on the elves." She scurried across the room, darting behind a rack of green and red candy-cane-striped costumes. Once she was out of sight, she leaned back against the wall and closed her eyes.

It's just a stupid crush. You'll get over it.

It didn't matter that she'd been telling herself the same thing for over a year. At some point it would be true, right?

It had to be.

Caleb's chest burned as he folded robe after robe and shoved them into one of the oversized trash bags, his skin beneath his black clerical shirt singed from where Molly's hands had lingered. She was avoiding finishing their conversation from the diner, steering them to topics of the weather or the specials menu at Lemon and Thyme or other equally inconsequential things every time he tried to get them back on track. He didn't want to spend the rest of the day with this awful weight in the pit of his stomach, this dread that they weren't understanding each other when he'd come to think of her as one of the people who understood him best.

But she clearly wasn't going to allow them to hash it out, which sent confusing ripples of something hot and primal through his blood. Something demanding he hold her still and make her understand. Something he definitely couldn't do anything about, so instead he shoved another lamb onesie roughly into the garbage bag at his feet.

The sooner they finished packing up the costumes and went home, the better. But they couldn't get back to Aster Bay without spending another three hours together, alone, in his car. What had he been thinking, letting her join him?

You weren't. And now you'll have to spend the rest of the week repenting for all the unholy thoughts you've had today.

And yet, it wasn't the unholy fantasies that troubled him most.

"Back at the diner," he began, his voice cutting through the quiet that had settled over them as they worked, "you were angry with me."

She set aside the shepherd's outfit she'd been folding and blinked up at him. "I'm sorry. I—"

"I'm not looking for an apology. I want to know why."

Molly seemed to consider this as she finished with the shepherd's outfit, placing it into an oversized trash bag already full-to-bursting with costumes. When he'd begun to think she might not answer him, she said, "I wasn't *mad* at you. I don't understand you."

The confession felt fragile, gossamer thin, like if he looked at it head on, he'd spook her and she wouldn't say any more. And he *had* to know more. So he reached for another angel costume and took his time folding it, keeping Molly in his peripheral vision as he worked. "What don't you understand?"

"You became a priest because you wanted to help kids who were lost feel loved instead."

It stung like an accusation. "I did. I still do."

"And yet you chose an institution that consistently tells kids who they are is wrong."

"That's not what we're trying to do—"

"Dennis O'Brien." She said the name like a curse, and he struggled to place it. "Briana Murphy." When he didn't seem to be getting it, she threw up her hands in frustration, exhaling harshly. "Alex Lambert."

The name of the current high school senior shook something loose in his brain and he realized each name she'd given him had been a student at St. Anthony's at some point in the recent past. "I'm not following," he said.

"All of those kids, and countless others, are tortured by the idea that their Church—their *God*—doesn't love them as they are."

She might as well have slapped him, the words landing like a blow he hadn't expected. "Why?"

"Come on, Caleb," she scoffed. "Dennis was suspended his junior year."

"He chose to withdraw and enroll in the public high school instead of returning for his senior year," he said, the story coming back to him.

"But why was he suspended in the first place?" she pushed, her eyes blazing with a mix of indignation and withheld tears.

"I...I don't know. Bruce handles all the suspensions. I—"

"He was suspended for kissing another boy in the school parking lot. It took more than a month after he came back before he would even speak in class, and then he was gone. Briana Murphy wouldn't sign a pro-life petition circulated in her religion class. She told her guidance counselor—in confidence—that she'd been driving other girls from the school to Planned Parenthood when they needed services and were too afraid to ask their parents for help. Bruce—"

"Called her parents." Caleb dragged his fingers over his closed eyelids. "I remember."

"And you did nothing while she was treated like a criminal."

He dropped his hands, helpless in the face of her disappointment. "The principal is in charge of disciplinary action."

"Even when that disciplinary action is a punishment for disagreeing with the Church? That's the behavior of a dictator."

How could he make her understand? It wasn't that he always agreed with Bruce—in fact, most of the time he strongly disagreed—but that wasn't the point. They were both cogs in the same machine and they each had their part to play. "It's not my place to tell Bruce how to do his job."

"Then whose place is it?" She shook her head, dashing away a tear from the corner of her eye before it could fall. "Those kids have enough to deal with without also wondering if they've betrayed God simply by existing. And your Church, the people deputized to spread its teachings amongst vulnerable *kids*, they aren't concerned with helping those kids feel loved. Only with their obedience."

"I don't care about *obedience*." The word was ash in his mouth.

"But you don't stop it. You're the only one who can and—"

He loosed a bitter laugh. "You think I have far more influence than I do."

"You said you wanted to serve God by loving His people, but I can't imagine a God who would want His people to feel the way your Church has made those kids feel. So who are you serving, Caleb? When you stand by and let Bruce Day terrorize our students for daring to not conform to the most hateful of the Church's teachings, who are you serving then?"

Each accusation pierced his skin, like shards of glass embedding themselves in sinew and muscle, a scrape he would remember each time he pressed on the spot. It's not that he hadn't known about the incidents she flung at him, but maybe he hadn't fully considered their implications, the ways in which his silence had become complicity.

He'd always comforted himself that the more regressive teachings of the Church were outweighed by the good, but for the students she'd named, there was no such balance. And if even one of those students felt less loved because of the teachings he'd devoted his life to, could that wrong ever actually be balanced out?

"And Alex Lambert?" he asked, his throat raw.

"Alex Lambert has been getting detention every day because he refuses to remove a rainbow flag pin from his backpack. If he gets one more week of detentions, he'll be ineligible for Valedictorian."

He shook his head, slashing his hand through the air. "No. Withholding the recognition of our best student's academic achievements for uniform violations is too petty even for Bruce."

"Is it?" She leaned against the heater at the edge of the room, the disappointment in her eyes so much worse than her anger. "You know the worst part? Alex wears that pin so other students know he is a safe place for them. Bruce told him it wouldn't be enough to remove the pin. He needed to repent and beg for God's forgiveness. But what should he be asking for forgiveness *for*? For being a good friend? For daring to show kindness to someone the Church has deemed a sinner?"

"That's not—He can't—Why didn't I know this?" Caleb stammered, his stomach roiling.

"I don't know, Father. How have you turned a blind eye to the harm being done in God's name all these years?"

"The Church has made mistakes. *I* have made mistakes." He held her gaze, pleading with her for the absolution he hadn't realized he needed. "But surely the good I've done outweighs the harm?"

"I don't know." She sounded so small and helpless he wanted to wrap her in his arms, to comfort them both with the physical closeness he had no right to desire. "How can you stand it? The hypocrisy, the hatefulness disguised as love. That's *not* love, Caleb."

"I know." The fierceness of his reply startled them both, and something seemed to settle in her eyes.

"You could love so big, Caleb, if you'd stop letting the Church tell you how."

"You two are still here?" Caleb looked up to see Father David in the doorway to the classroom. "I thought you would have left at least an hour ago."

Caleb glanced around the room. It was mostly packed in boxes and bags now, the racks standing empty, but he hardly saw any of it, his mind spinning with the things Molly had said. Guilt congealed in his stomach, mingling with a longing for something he was afraid to name. "We must have lost track of time."

"You better get moving. The snow's coming down hard now."

Chapter Five

With Father David's help, Molly and Caleb loaded their car with as much as it could hold, which turned out to only be a fraction of what they'd packed. The snow was already deep enough to tug at Caleb's shoes, his feet sinking in up to the middle of his calf as they moved between the school and the car, soaking the lower half of his pant legs. Molly did an admirable job of trying to clear the windshield, but for every swath of snow she cleared, more fell, faster and harder by the second. Off in the distance, the streetlights were hazy in the white glow of the snow. Caleb could hardly see the end of the school's driveway.

Molly cleared the same area of the windshield for the third time, then dropped the scraper to her side, worry pulling at the corner of her mouth. "We can't drive in this."

His heart pounded. "I'm sure it will be fine once we get on the highway."

Father David re-emerged from the school with the last garbage bag and handed it off to Caleb to place in the backseat. "Bad news, I'm afraid. I just got an alert the highway's closed to all but essential vehicles."

Fear slithered beneath Caleb's skin. What had he gotten them into? "Then we'll take backroads."

"Those will be worse. White out conditions." Father David flipped the collar of his jacket up against the biting wind and driving snow. "I think you two are stuck in Nativity for a while, Father."

"No, we can't—"

"We have a spare room here in the rectory, but I think you'd be more comfortable at the motel. It's less than a mile down the road. If you leave now and go slow, you can get there before the wind kicks up and makes it any harder to see. Just look for the star."

"A motel," Caleb repeated. His face was numb in the frigid air.

"Go now, my friend. Stay safe."

Caleb watched Father David retreat back towards the school, ducking his head as snow pelted him from all sides.

"Caleb."

Blood rushed in his ears and he flexed his fingers in the pockets of his too-thin jacket. They'd go to the motel, they'd rent two rooms and ride out the storm, and in the morning, when the roads were clear, they'd drive home and everything would be fine. It was *fine*. It was just a little snow.

Or maybe it's a sign...

Of what? My inability to check a weather forecast?

"Father West! We have to go." The rising panic in Molly's voice snapped him out of his trance and he gave a curt nod before joining her in the car, the heat blasting and the wipers working overtime to keep his view clear.

Snow crunched beneath the tires as he carefully steered the car out of the parking lot and onto the deserted road. They moved at a snail's pace, his attempts to keep the car from fishtailing on the slippery road at odds with his desire to move faster, to get them out of harm's way—to get *her* out of harm's way. A gentle curve in the road felt like a roller coaster, each bend more treacherous than the last, until, at last, a giant, neon yellow, glowing star in the distance came into view.

"Follow the star," he muttered.

The Starshine Motel was one of those two-story roadside motels Caleb had only seen in movies, with a whitewashed cement façade and a steel railing running along the second story walkway. Each door was hung with an identical wreath and, beneath the sign with its neon star, was a nativity scene populated by plastic snowmen slowly being buried in the falling snow. The car slid to a stop in the parking lot, snow coming down so hard and fast now it was hard to make out where the other cars were beneath the blanket of white.

"I shouldn't have said anything. About the Church," Molly said when Caleb had parked the car. "I made it weird."

"I'm glad you said something." At her little sound of disbelief, he reached across the center console and gripped her hand. "Are we okay?"

"We're okay."

She opened her mouth like she wanted to say something else, but the snow had already coated the windshield in the few moments they'd sat in the parking lot. Despite the warmth rushing through him at her gentle reassurance, the voice in the back of his mind demanded he get her inside, get her warm, get her *safe*.

He squeezed her hand and reluctantly pulled away. "We should go in, before we get stuck out here."

The small rental office was empty when Molly and Caleb pushed through the front doors, kicking snow from their shoes. The light from a low ceiling fan cast the modest wood-paneled room in an orange glow. A bell over the door announced their arrival and a woman in her mid-70s with a short, gray bob looked up from the Harlequin romance she was reading at the check-in desk.

"What are you folks doing out in this storm?" she gasped, dropping her book. "Come in, come in. Are you the couple in 3B?"

"What? No," Molly sputtered. "Us? We're not—we're not a couple."

Caleb did his best to block out the restless, staticky feeling pulsing through his veins at the mere idea of being mistaken for Molly's partner and the sick weight turning over in his stomach from their last conversation. "It seems we chose the wrong day to road trip to Nativity. I don't suppose you have a couple of rooms open for the night?"

The woman's face fell. "No, I'm sorry, we don't. My last room was booked just a few hours ago."

Molly laughed, a brittle, hysterical sound. "You've got to be kidding me. We followed the star and there's no room at the inn! I think I've heard this story before." She jabbed a finger at the sky, her voice high pitched. "Joke's on you, God! I haven't been a virgin since high school!"

"Oh, my," the woman said, glancing between them.

Caleb pressed a hand to Molly's lower back and she sucked in a breath, turning her wild eyes towards him, but he was determined to ignore the way that small sound sent heat racing down his spine. With his free hand, he lowered the zipper on his jacket, just enough to reveal his clerical collar. The woman's eyes zeroed in on the square of white like a homing beacon.

"Is there anything you can do for us? My friend and I just need a safe space to ride out the storm," he said.

The woman thought for a moment, glancing uncertainly out the window at her back. "There is The Stable."

Another incredulous puff of laughter burst from Molly's lips before she clapped her hand over her mouth.

"It's the renovated barn out back. We use it as a vacation rental home." The woman pointed out the window to a cabin set a little way back on the property, barely visible through the swirling storm. "It was supposed to be rented out all weekend for a bachelor party, but they called yesterday and cancelled." She dropped her voice and leaned closer. "Apparently the bride and the best man were having a thing on the side." Her eyes flashed to Caleb's clerical collar again and she cleared her throat, straightening her spine. "The house is fully stocked and sitting there empty. I could give it to you for the cost of a standard room, seeing how it'll just be going to waste otherwise, if you don't mind the bachelor party décor."

"That would be incredibly generous of you..."

"Mary."

"Mary," Caleb repeated with a strained smile.

Someone up there has a sick sense of humor.

The Stable may have been a barn once, but there was only the barest hint of that history remaining in the large, open concept cabin. The wide-plank hardwood floors, exposed beams, and large stone fireplace with its barnwood mantle gave the space a rustic vibe at odds with the luxury furniture and stainless-steel appliances in the kitchen. When Caleb and Molly burst through the front door, a flurry of snow followed them inside and covered the welcome mat. It had been a treacherous trudge from the motel to the cabin through the rapidly accumulating snow dunes, and Molly's fingers stung as newfound warmth thawed her frozen extremities.

"Take off your shoes," Caleb said.

Molly pulled her attention away from the wall of windows at the back of the living room overlooking a stretch of forest blanketed in white to find Caleb sitting on the small wooden bench just inside the front door, untying his sneakers.

"They're soaked through, Molly. We need to get out of these wet clothes. Take off your shoes before your feet freeze."

"Right, of course."

She sat down next to him and untied her shoes, ignoring the way her thigh brushed against his. That wasn't a helpful thing to notice in a time like this, not when there was this weird tension between them since she'd scolded him back at the school, and especially not when Caleb's eyes seemed to be locked on her feet. Her bright green socks featured a shirtless Santa, suspenders framing his six-pack abs. They'd been a Christmas gift from Jo last year and, when she'd put them on that morning, they'd made her giggle. Now, she couldn't peel them off her wet feet fast enough.

"I knew you couldn't be a grinch. No one who hates Christmas would own those socks," Caleb teased lightly, as though he was testing if it was still okay to.

"I never said I hate Christmas." Molly stomped over to the fireplace, wet socks balled in her hands. Mary had mentioned the fireplace was gas. If she could just find the 'on' switch, they could warm up faster, but there didn't seem to be any buttons hidden in the stonework.

Suddenly, the fire roared to life and Molly spun around to find Caleb aiming a remote at the fireplace. "So is it just depictions of Jesus' birth you take issue with or—"

"They were inflatable lobsters! What exactly is Christ-like about inflatable crustaceans?"

Caleb laughed, his Adam's apple bobbing above his clerical collar. "Nothing at all," he conceded. "Nothing *Christ-like* about horny Santa socks, either."

Molly threw the wadded up wet socks at him, smiling. "I don't know. Jesus was a carpenter. I bet that man had abs for days."

He blinked. "Did you just...objectify the Lord?" She told herself the heat overtaking her face was because of her proximity to the fireplace. Caleb shook his head and tossed the socks back at her. "Never mind. Don't answer that."

She should let it drop, but as she followed him up the staircase to the bedrooms where Mary had promised they'd find dry bathrobes and slippers, she couldn't help but needle him. "Is it my preference for secular Christmas iconography that bothers you, or is it the idea Santa can be sexy?"

"Santa can be whatever you want. *Santa's* not real."

Molly gasped in mock shock. "How can you say he's not real when we have at least twenty of his outfits in the back of your car?"

Something flashed behind Caleb's eyes and his darkened gaze flitted over her form, the same heated look he'd given her back at the school when she'd held up the Santa dress. If she'd blinked, she might have missed the way his throat bobbed on his upward sweep of her body, a ruddy color spreading over his cheekbones. He threw open the closet door at her side, and pulled out two white terrycloth robes, his expression clearing as he carefully removed them from their hangers.

"I'll change in the other room." He handed her a robe before disappearing back into the hallway, pulling the bedroom door closed behind him and leaving Molly with a hot, staticky feeling prickling along the path his eyes had taken.

Molly stripped off her shirt and shimmied out of her jeans, the lower half of which were completely soaked from their trek through the snow. Thankfully, her bra and panties were dry and the robe was soft and warm against her skin. She shot off a quick text to Jo to let her know she wouldn't be making it back to their shared apartment that night.

> **Jo:** You're snowed in?? Please tell me there's only one bed.

> **Molly:** There are plenty of beds. I think this place has something like six bedrooms.

> **Jo:** Well, that's disappointing.

Molly rolled her eyes.

> **Molly:** It's just one night. Once the storm clears, we'll be back on the road in the morning.

Jo: You have to tell me what Father West looks like with his shirt off. I bet he's got one of those muscle V's pointing to his dick.

Molly: I will not be seeing Caleb with his shirt off. How would that even happen?

Jo: I don't know. Spill a drink on him. Get creative. Horny former Catholic school girls everywhere are counting on you!

Molly: Good night, Jo. I'll text you when we get on the road tomorrow.

Jo: Have fun being snowed in with the hot priest. Don't do anything I wouldn't do.

Molly: There's nothing you wouldn't do.

Jo: Exactly *wink emoji*

Chapter Six

C aleb stared at the variety of frozen pizzas stuffed into the freezer, but he hardly registered what he was looking at. Somewhere upstairs Molly Proulx was taking off her clothes. She was removing her clothing in the same building he was in, getting ready to put on the same absurdly soft robe he was wearing. He'd almost kept his shirt on, despite the wet spots where the snow had slipped beneath his jacket, just to feel the collar at his throat, the reminder of all the reasons he should not be thinking about Molly Proulx undressing, or that feral demand whispering in the back of his brain. In the end, the cold had won out and he'd bundled his shirt in the dryer in the laundry room along with the rest of his clothing. There was something thrilling about standing in the kitchen in just his boxer briefs and a robe, waiting for Molly to come downstairs—thrilling and yet somehow peaceful. Domestic in a way he never thought he'd experience.

You're trapped by a snowstorm, not playing house. Stop romanticizing it.

The bottom step of the staircase creaked as Molly descended, and Caleb forced himself to keep his eyes on the pizza boxes. "Apparently frozen pizzas are the food of choice for bachelor parties. What are you in the mood for—pepperoni or Hawaiian?"

"You choose."

He was aware of her moving around the kitchen behind him as he selected a box of pepperoni pizza and preheated the oven, the soft sound of her bare feet landing on the hardwood floor, the click as she opened a cabinet and then closed it again. He wondered if she'd left her underwear on beneath her robe, if she'd added her clothing to the dryer with his, their clothes tangling together in ways their bodies never would.

Stop.

She opened another cabinet and reached for something at the back, rising up on her tip toes. The move highlighted the muscle in her calf beneath the hem of her robe, and his eyes lingered there, mapping the strength beneath her skin. She pulled a giant tub of hot cocoa mix from the cabinet and set it on the counter with a triumphant smile.

"There's another nativity scene in the hall outside the bathroom upstairs," she said, reaching back into the cabinet.

He set the frozen pizza on a sheet pan and slid it into the open oven, still pre-heating. "What's this one, rubber duckies?"

"Nope," she said, popping the 'p' and setting a large bottle of Kahlua next to the cocoa mix. She turned and leaned against the counter, her hands trapped between her back and the butcher block, and a shy grin stole over her face. "Cookie cutters. Gingerbread men—and women. It's not very family friendly."

Caleb's brow furrowed. "What does that mean?"

"Let's just say the Virgin Mary is most definitely not a virgin in this particular scene. It's more like gingerbread men gone wild, plus baby Jesus. I think it may be part of the bachelor party decor we were warned about. Hot cocoa?"

He struggled to keep up with the change of topic, his mind trying to piece together how a nativity scene could be considered bachelor party decor. "Sure. No alcohol in mine."

"Suit yourself." She filled the tea kettle and set it on the stove. Then, as though something had just occurred to her, she furrowed her brow. "Are priests not allowed to drink?"

"You've seen me drink before. I have a beer at family dinner sometimes."

She opened her mouth as though she were going to fire back some kind of witty retort, but then she closed it without speaking and turned away, retrieving mugs from the cabinet by the sink. Again, she was up on her toes, searching for the handles just out of her reach.

"I've got it." Caleb moved behind her, resting one hand low on her back as he reached around her with the other to retrieve the mugs from the top shelf. He wanted to linger with his palm against her back, to feel her body shift beneath the fabric, but he made himself set the mug on the counter and take a step away, putting some much needed distance between them. "I'm allowed to drink," he said, his eyes drifting back to her ankles like he was some kind of repressed aristocrat in a Jane Austen novel. "I just don't think it's a very good idea for me to drink tonight."

She seemed to consider this as she poured the boiling water into the mugs and stirred heaping spoonfuls of chocolatey powder mix into each. "Is it going to make you uncomfortable if I drink?"

He shook his head. "Have at it. I'm pretty sure there's more booze in this place than food anyway."

She screwed her lips up to the side as she considered the bottle of Kahlua on the counter. "It feels weird to be the only one drinking."

He shouldn't do it. He should take his hot cocoa, wait for the frozen pizza to finish cooking, and call it an early night, lock himself away in the bedroom farthest from hers and spend the night in silent prayer and reflection.

He should do anything other than grab the bottle of Kahlua and add a healthy pour to each of their mugs. He shouldn't be delighted by her lips curling into a smile and the sparkle in her eyes, and he definitely shouldn't be wondering what else he could do to put that look on her face.

"Don't bend the rules on my account," she said, though her grin made it clear she liked it when he bent the rules.

But this wasn't a big rule, not an *official* rule—and really, he wasn't a big fan of the official rules lately anyway. It was more of his own personal guideline. *Don't get drunk with the woman who already tests your self-control.*

It seemed like a reasonable rule, until she looked at him with that glimmer in her eyes.

"You are a bad influence," he scolded as he lifted his mug to his lips.

"Excuse me, sir, I will have you know I am an amazing influence." As if to challenge her own point, she added more Kahlua to her mug.

His lip twitched as he fought to contain his smile. "Is that so?"

"Jo says I'm the mom of our friend group."

"That's because Jo is a chaos demon."

Her laugh warmed him far more than the spiked hot chocolate.

They wandered into the living room and took seats on opposite ends of the couch in front of the fireplace. She turned towards him, tucking her foot up under herself, and he did his best not to notice the way her robe shifted, or the tempting glimpses of her skin it offered.

Thankfully her gaze was focused on the windows behind him so she didn't notice his wandering eyes as they hungrily took in the flash of lace at the edge of her robe before the delicate pattern gave way to shadow. The wind howled outside, a mournful, haunted sound, and the lights flickered.

"It's really coming down out there," she said, her voice quiet and small.

He glanced over his shoulder at the snow-covered landscape, then back at Molly, who seemed to be shrinking in on herself. There were so many ways their day trip could have gone wrong today... Without thinking, he reached across the couch and laid his hand on top of hers. "We're safe. It's okay."

She shivered again, her eyes zeroing in on his fingers sweeping comforting arcs over the back of her hand. Her skin was so smooth, so warm. He should stop touching her, but...he didn't want to.

"I will never let anything bad happen to you, Molly," he promised. It was the easiest vow he'd ever made.

She nodded, the promise settling between them. "We should play a game," she said at last, gently pulling her hand away from his and wrapping it around her mug.

"What kind of game?"

"A slumber party game. Like Two Truths and a Lie, or Never Have I Ever."

"This isn't exactly a slumber party."

"Not with that attitude it isn't."

He settled back against the arm of the couch, putting a little more distance between them. He should say no, but he had to admit he was intrigued. "Truth or Dare."

"I'm warning you now, I almost always choose truth."

"Why's that?"

"Because you could dare me to do anything! And I'm not about to ask Jenny Barber's older brother to kiss me twice in one lifetime. Fool me once," she said, shaking her head.

Something cold congealed in Caleb's stomach, and he knew he shouldn't ask, but he couldn't help it. Now he had to know. "And did he?"

"Did who what?"

"Did Jenny Barber's brother kiss you?"

She studied him for a moment over the top of her mug as she took a slow sip of her hot chocolate. "He laughed in my face and told me to move so he could see the TV. Though, to be fair, he was in college and I was only thirteen, so in retrospect, not exactly the jerk I thought he was at the time."

Caleb exhaled harshly through his nose, relief flooding through him. Which was ridiculous, because of course Molly had kissed people before, even if she hadn't kissed Jenny Barber's older brother when she was thirteen. "Anyone else you almost-kissed on a dare that I should know about?"

She arched an eyebrow at him as though she saw straight through his irrational jealousy and found it amusing. "No, but I definitely made out with a guy at a party on a dare."

"Who was he?" He didn't want to know, and yet he might die if she didn't tell him.

"It was a long time ago."

"Can't have been that long." She was only twenty-six after all.

"My college boyfriend. Will."

"Did you love him?" He didn't know why it mattered. Molly had been single as long as he'd known her, but somehow it mattered very much.

She looked off into the distance as she considered her words. Caleb didn't know this Will person, but he didn't like him already. "We were young."

"That's not what I asked."

"It was college. He was a year older and in one of Kyla's photography classes. An artist. Passionate, broody. You know the type." He did, and he'd never been so jealous in his life. "Anyway, like I said, we were young."

"What happened?" He hated himself for asking.

"He got offered a scholarship for grad school in California and he said he'd turn it down if I wanted him to." She shrugged, unable to hide the grimace at the memory. "I thought it was romantic. I thought we were in love. But really, as time went on, it became clear he resented me for asking him to stay. The regret...it broke us. Maybe we would have broken anyway."

"He didn't deserve you."

"You didn't know him."

"I know you."

She looked away, and cleared her throat, the sound breaking whatever spell he'd been under. "What about you, Father? Truth or Dare?"

"I also always pick Truth," he admitted.

"So what you're telling me is we're really playing Twenty Questions. I can work with that." She shifted on the couch and her robe slid open further at her neckline, just enough to give him a glimpse of her clavicle, the small cluster of freckles at the edge of her neckline above the swell of her breasts.

Stop thinking about her breasts.

He took a sip of his hot chocolate and focused his attention on the heat of the mug seeping into his palms. "We could pick another game," he offered.

"Nope. Too late. I already have my first question."

He bit back a smile. "Then by all means."

"Favorite Christmas tradition?" she asked.

"When I was a kid, we used to make gingerbread houses every year. Gavin and I would each get to choose what kind of house we wanted to make. We were supposed to pick something to represent our hopes for the coming year. My mom would spend days baking all the pieces. She made templates from Cheerios boxes and kept them in the junk drawer in the kitchen," he said, chuckling. "I haven't thought about those in years. The week before Christmas, we'd go to the store and buy all the candy we could carry and then we'd spend a whole night assembling and decorating while we listened to the John Denver Muppet Christmas album on vinyl on repeat."

She settled against the back of the couch, leaning a bit closer to him. "What was your favorite house?"

"The year we made the farm. Hands down. Gavin made the farmhouse, and I made the barn. Mom even cut out pieces to make a grain silo and cows and sheep. We used shredded wheat bricks for hay bales and pretzel rods to build a fence around the pasture, and so much red icing. When it was done, Mom said she wasn't sure what dream we were trying to manifest, but the best she could do was a trip to Longfield Farm in the spring." He paused, a bittersweet happiness settling over him at the memory. "We haven't done it since I left for college."

"Why not? You should revive the tradition!"

"We're adults now—"

"You're adults who get together with your friends to play competitive games of Monopoly and Uno. I think you could make gingerbread houses without worrying about it being too childish."

He laughed. "You have a point." He took the last sip of his hot cocoa and, as he placed the empty mug on the coffee table, wondered if the warmth flowing through his extremities was because of the fireplace, the alcohol, or her.

"I've never made a gingerbread house," she admitted.

"You haven't? I thought everyone made them as kids."

"Just the ones with graham crackers and milk cartons you make in elementary school. My mom made amazing gingerbread cookies, but we weren't allowed to make houses from them. She said it was wasteful."

"Then that settles it. We'll have to revive the tradition when we get back to Aster Bay. Everyone should make at least one gingerbread house in their lifetime."

"Think we can convince the gang to forego a board game night in favor of gingerbread?"

"Not a chance," he said, "But I think we can convince them to tack it onto the next game night."

"Sounds like a plan. I might even try making my mom's recipe. I haven't made it in years."

He twisted to face her more fully. "What's your favorite Christmas tradition?"

"When I was little, every year on Christmas Eve, my dad and I would lie on the floor under the Christmas tree and he would read me *Santa Mouse*. Do you know it?"

"No, I can't say I do."

"It's a children's picture book about a mouse who doesn't have any family or even a name. He puts out a piece of cheese for Santa on Christmas Eve and Santa is so moved by it, he gives the mouse a name and invites him to join him on his journey to deliver presents." She smiled to herself as she finished her hot cocoa and set the mug down. "Every year, we'd read the book and then we'd put out cookies for Santa and a little piece of cheese for Santa Mouse, but not the slices of American cheese or blocks of cheddar we usually had in the fridge. Dad would go to the store and buy a wedge of brie or gouda or Manchego. Something special. The pine needles would fall into the cheese and we'd steal little slices off the edge while Dad read. But then I got older and we stopped reading and Mom got tired of vacuuming up the pine needles. I don't think I've had a real Christmas tree since I was a teenager." She paused, and when she spoke again, it was as though she were speaking to herself and not him. "Someday, I'm going to buy fancy cheese and read books to my kids under a real Christmas tree."

His heart thudded painfully at the idea of Molly with children, with a husband, a family he had no part of. "You'll be an amazing mom."

"Did you ever want kids? Before you..." She waved her hand at him as though that completed her sentence.

"I was only twenty when I began my formation." He scrubbed a hand over the back of his neck and glanced away. "Honestly, before that, I was more concerned with *not* getting a girl pregnant."

She gasped, her eyes widening, and pressed a mock-scandalized hand to her chest. "Father West, are you not a virgin?"

He wanted to press his lips to the hollow of her throat. "I am not, Ms. Proulx."

"Damn." She let out a slow breath as she melted back against the couch, leaning her head back even as she kept her eyes on him. "I really wish I didn't know that."

His skin buzzed, electrified by her nearness and the distracting sliver of skin at her neckline and the soft sort of longing in her voice—or had he imagined that?

If he were any other man, he would reach across the space between them and trace her smile with his tongue. He'd let the desire and frustration clouding his senses take over. It would be the most natural thing in the world to kiss her, to touch her. Far more so than the immense effort he was expending to stay on his side of the couch. But when she looked at him like that, her eyes warm and a little sad, like she *knew* exactly how wonderful they could be together and had already mourned the impossibility of it, when she looked at him like she saw the man beneath the vestments, like she cared for him not because of his vocation but perhaps in spite of it...

If he were any other man, he could make her happy. He was sure of it.

"I guess I always assumed, in order to give something like that up, you must never have experienced it," she said.

The standard reply was out of his mouth before he'd even really considered it. "Sexuality is such a small part of who we are."

"But don't you ever miss it? Sometimes I just need to be touched, to connect with another person."

"You can have connection without taking your clothes off," he said, though his skin had heated at her words, desire washing over him. *Careful.* "We're connecting right now."

She shook her head. "That's different. That's— Oh." She broke off, as though she'd solved some hidden puzzle. "I see."

"What do you see, Ms. Proulx?" he asked, a teasing lilt slipping into his tone.

"Nothing. Forget it," she said, sitting up straight.

"Say it. Unless you're choosing dare?" He arched an eyebrow at her expectantly.

"Dare," she whispered.

"I dare you to tell me."

He could practically see the wheels turning in her head, the debate she was having with herself. At last, she looked him dead in the eyes, and said, "You may not be a virgin, but you've never had good sex."

"I have had plenty of—"

She barreled on, a lift at the corner of her lips as though she had him all figured out. "Not just sex that feels good, but sex that rewrites your DNA."

All teasing fell away. "What do you mean?"

She closed her eyes, her hands hovering over her heart, as she spoke. "Being with someone like that, it's not just because you're chasing a release. You're inviting them to become a part of you. When you can't get close enough, and they become a part of every cell, rewiring every atom. When each touch, each breath, grounds you more in your body. Somehow, being as close to another person as physically possible becomes about so much more than bodies. It's recognizing the light in another person, understanding that alone we aren't complete..." She opened her eyes, sighing dreamily. "Sex like that... I can't imagine giving that up."

He struggled to swallow, his throat constricted. "And you have had sex like that?"

The sadness in her eyes at whatever memory she was recalling broke his heart and made him unreasonably jealous all at the same time. "Almost. Once. But I believe I'll find it again, and this time I'll get to keep it."

In the other room, the oven timer dinged. Caleb cleared his throat and got to his feet, suddenly hot and itchy all over, like his skin was too tight. "That'll be our dinner," he mumbled as he hurried from the room, her words echoing in his mind.

She was right. He'd never had sex like that. The fumblings of his teenage years hadn't prepared him for the possibility sex could be more than a physical give and take, but his blood hummed in recognition as she'd spoken. An involuntary acknowledgment of the truth in her words, a painful awareness of this entire aspect of human existence he had never experienced, would never experience—and why? How did this sacrifice, this artificial constraint on his humanity, glorify God?

What if the Church was wrong?

He closed his eyes and pressed his hands over his heart as Molly had done, breathing into the ache behind his sternum, the emptiness growing day after day, the loneliness no amount of prayer had assuaged. What if all this time the problem hadn't been his faith or his temptations? What if sex wasn't merely a biological impulse, but was actually the greatest moment of connection—to each other *and* to God—man could experience in this life?

And what if Caleb wanted to experience it too?

Chapter Seven

M olly couldn't sleep.

It wasn't just the strange bed or the light from the small bedside lamp (so much brighter than the one she left on at night in her bedroom at home) or the howling wind as it whipped around their cabin, threatening to tear it clean off its foundation. She was restless, her limbs vibrating with the intensity of her attraction to Caleb, with the belated embarrassment from their last conversation. Dinner had been eaten in strained silence before they'd said an early goodnight and shuffled off to their respective bedrooms, and it was all her fault.

I can't believe I told Caleb he hasn't had good sex.

She couldn't stop thinking about what it would be like to have sex with Caleb. It didn't matter that he was her frolleague, or twenty years older than her, or even that he was a priest. She wanted him. And she was pretty sure he wanted her too. Somehow she knew with a bone-deep knowing, sex with Caleb would be everything she'd described downstairs and more.

In the dark, she let her hand drift across her collar bone, fingertips grazing the sensitive skin, before sliding down to skate over her breasts. Her nipples pulled tight beneath the lace of her bra, and she continued her slow path over the peaks, across the soft roundness of her stomach, until her fingers danced at the waistband of her panties.

It was wrong to touch herself while she thought about him.

Not that that's stopped you before.

But he isn't usually in the next room.

A tree branch groaned beneath the weight of the falling snow outside her window, the wind loud enough he'd never hear her. He'd never have to know...

She wriggled out of her panties and dropped them on the floor beside the bed. Her robe fell open beneath the heavy comforter, and she drew her fingers through her wetness. In slow strokes, she teased herself, never touching where she wanted it most. Where she wanted him.

A loud crack and the room plunged into darkness, the whirring of the heating system abruptly halting.

"Shit," she whispered, pulling her hand away and fumbling on the nightstand for the remote to the fireplace on the other side of the room. She only succeeded in knocking her cell phone onto the floor. With a muttered curse, she sat up in bed, turning her attention fully to the task at hand.

"You're okay," she mumbled to herself. "You are a full-grown adult with a job and a lease and crushing student loan debt. Full-grown adults are not afraid of the dark."

The door to her bedroom flew open, a single point of too-bright light temporarily blinding her and she sucked in a startled breath. "Are you alright?" Caleb asked, his voice rough. Though he was hard to see in the shadow of his cell phone flashlight, she could tell he was more disheveled than usual, his robe hanging open on his shoulders as though he'd thrown it on in a hurry and his hair sticking up in all directions.

"I'm fine. I can't find the remote for the fireplace."

He stalked across the room and found the button beneath the mantle. A fire roared to life in the fireplace, limning him in flame. He turned back to her, his eyes dragging along the opening of her robe, but she couldn't bring herself to close it. His eyes on her made warmed her more than any fire could.

He swallowed, his Adam's apple bobbing in his throat. "That should keep you warm until the power comes back on." His eyes traced her form one more time, then he cleared his throat and turned towards the door.

"Do you have a fireplace in your room?" she asked.

He shook his head. "I'll sleep on the couch near the one in the living room."

Something wild fluttered in her chest in protest, a desperate need to say something—anything—to make him stay. If she didn't say something now, then would she ever?

She scooted over in the bed and flipped back the corner of the comforter. "Or you could stay here."

His face was hard, unreadable in the dim, flickering light of the fire, and he stood so still, like an animal hiding from a predator. *Or like the predator itself.*

"I'm not sure that's a good idea."

"What, do you snore or something?" she asked, the poor attempt at a joke falling flat.

"Molly..." The grit in his voice sent electricity down her spine.

"I don't like the dark," she admitted. "As in, I hate it." Even with his face half in shadow, she felt his eyes on her. "Please stay."

At last, he crossed the room to the bedside and sat gingerly on the edge of the mattress. He slid beneath the covers, careful not to touch her. His breathing was somehow louder than the wind outside, the heat radiating from him making her almost too warm, and yet she wouldn't have said so for all the world.

"Why do you hate the dark?" His voice rumbled through her, low and reassuring even though it was difficult to see his face.

"I don't know. I just always have. I get these nightmares that seem so real and—" She shook off the thought. "Never mind. It's silly."

"It's not silly to me."

His words settled over her like a weighted blanket. "The nightmares are bad enough, but when I wake up from them, if I can't see where I am, if I don't know I'm safe, it's hard to make myself believe it was just a dream."

Another crack outside tore through the night air and she let out a yelp of surprise, pushing back against him, her back to his front, as though she could get away from the sounds outside her window. As though just being near him could calm the sudden adrenaline rushing through her veins.

"Shhh," he crooned, gathering her against him. "I've got you."

She wrapped her arms around his, pulling him closer as she settled into his heat, his pine and sandalwood scent enveloping her. The scruff of his chin scraped at the place where her neck met her shoulder and she wondered how it would feel against other parts of her. A bolt of desire arrowed between her legs and she pressed her thighs together.

She held her breath and pushed back against him, her backside grinding against his groin and the unmistakable bulge of him pressed to her. A low rumble sounded in his throat as the bulge jolted, lengthened, and his fingertips slid into the opening of her robe, digging into her waist as he attempted to hold her still.

"Caleb."

His muscled thigh slid between her legs, pressing mercifully at the apex of her thighs. She shivered in his hold and pressed back, the pressure delicious and not nearly enough.

"Go to sleep, Molly," he said, his voice all gravel and command. As if she could sleep *now*. His thigh pressed against her tighter, holding her captive in a place of suspended desire. "Please."

If this was all she could have, one night in his arms, then she'd take it, knowing it would never be enough.

At some point she must have drifted off to sleep. When she woke in the darkness, shadows cast from the low fire across the room, Caleb was still there, his hands large and hot on her skin beneath her robe and his breath warm on her cheek. Their legs were still tangled and she rocked experimentally against his thigh, the need pulsing through her all-consuming. Could she come like this, with just his thigh to grind against?

She circled her hips, pleasure shooting through her at the added pressure, and she stifled a groan. Then she did it again. Each movement of her hips also had the unexpected but undeniably enticing side effect of pressing her ass against Caleb's erection. Another circle, another groan, this time of frustration. It wasn't enough. She needed more.

One of his hands, rough and warm, slid up her waist, his thumb brushing against the underside of her breast, the nail scratching lightly through the lace of her bra, and she stifled a gasp.

"Do that again," she whispered.

And he did. She melted into his touch, into the knowledge that he was touching her back.

"Caleb—"

"Shhh." He cut her off, his face buried in her hair, lips against her shoulder. "I've got you," he said, just as he'd said when he first climbed into bed.

"This doesn't feel real," she whispered into the dark.

Another slow swipe of his thumb. "Maybe it's not." His hand closed over hers, lacing his fingers with hers from behind, and he dragged her palm up to cup her own breast, his hand holding hers in place, directing her movement. His breath was hot against her ear. "Maybe I'm not even really here."

Together, they massaged her breast, his movements dictating hers, and she arched into the contact. "Maybe I'm dreaming," she offered.

He hummed, a deep, molten sound. His free hand closed over her free hand on her stomach, his fingertips dragging over the soft skin of her belly through her fingers. "Is this what you dream about, angel?"

The nickname skipped across her skin, like a stone across water, each point of connection a ripple of something electric and warm wrapping itself around her. She slid her hand lower, taking his with her, until they settled between her parted thighs. It was her own fingertip tracing her slit, her own finger slowly circling her clit, but it was his controlling the pace, the pressure. She was so wet already, her clit throbbing with the need to come, and she thought she really must be dreaming.

He rocked against her, grinding his cock against her ass in slow, unhurried movements, as though they had all the time in the world. As though this wasn't a stolen moment that never should have belonged to them.

Molly moved lower, sliding two fingers deep inside herself as his hold moved to her wrist, urging her on, but not touching her directly. Not really.

"In my dreams, you touch me," she said, near tears with want of it.

He grunted, a low rough sound, before his fingers dipped between her lips, tracing the place where her fingers disappeared inside her. "Here?" He moved to her clit, soft and rough all at once, pressing against her with firm circles that sent sparks shooting down her legs and across the soles of her feet. "Here?"

"There," she gasped, lifting her hips into his touch.

"Hmmm." The sound scraped at her skin. "I touch you here in my dreams too."

Her stomach tightened, pleasure gathering behind her clit with each brush of his fingers. Between his hands and her own, she was overcome with sensation, and yet she wanted more. "What else do you do in your dreams?" she asked.

He pinched her clit, hard, the sudden bite of pain heightening her pleasure. He thrust against her ass, his thick erection mimicking the movement of her own fingers inside her. "Everything."

Her orgasm took her by surprise, barreling into her, knocking the air from her lungs as she shook in his arms. He released her clit and resumed his slow, relentless circles, prolonging her climax. With a grunt and another hard thrust, his grinding at her back ceased, his breathing slowed, and she thought his lips whispered against her shoulder. He moved to withdraw his hand, but it was her turn to grip his wrist, to hold him in place.

"Not yet," she said, the words scraped raw. "It's just a dream."

The tension in his body eased and he shifted slightly so his palm cupped her between the legs, keeping her back tight against his front. "Just a dream," he agreed.

His other hand slid down to her waist, holding her so tightly she could hardly breathe, but she'd gladly stop breathing if she could keep this moment for a little longer. Another one of those whisper kisses, so light she'd wonder later if she'd imagined them.

"Go to sleep, angel."

Chapter Eight

December 23rd

He'd touched her.

He'd held her while she came—while he made her come—and then, grinding against her ass, he'd come in his boxer briefs.

And, Lord help him, he wanted to do it again.

There was no denying it, even to himself. Why should he when she'd liked it? And he *liked* that she liked it. He wanted to know what else she might like, how else he might make her tremble in his arms, the taste she would leave on his lips.

He'd woken in her bed, wrapped around her, his cock harder than it'd ever been and his nose buried in her hair, surrounded by the cinnamon and bergamot scent of her shampoo. At some point in the night, the power had come back on, but the fire continued burning in the fireplace across the room, its reflected glow making her look like the angel he'd called her. She'd shifted in her sleep, snuggling closer, his hands on her bare skin, and he'd panicked.

He wasn't proud of the way he'd stolen from her bed, of the prayers he'd tried to recite to himself as he showered, but the words hadn't come. All he could think about was how he didn't want to wash her scent from his skin, how he wanted to crawl back into her bed and never leave, how he wanted more stolen moments, more of the fantasy that he was the kind of man who could have a future with her. The kind of man who could wake up with her each morning, who could touch her without guilt.

Christ, he wanted to touch her again. To kiss her and taste her, to see her laid out before him and sink into her heat—

Enough. No wonder you couldn't pray this morning when you're behaving like a hormonal teenager.

Caleb welcomed the bracing cold as he threw open the back door of the cabin. In the mudroom closet he'd found a pair of snow pants, two sizes too big, and a pair of winter boots, at least two sizes too small, but they were better than freezing in his own inadequate clothing as he trudged through the snow. His glasses fogged up with the steam from his breath, but he couldn't be bothered with that now. At least he *had* his glasses since wearing day old contacts wasn't high on his list of things that made for a good time.

He hadn't planned on going outside in the aftermath of the storm, not until they were plowed out at least, but then he'd spotted the ax in the mudroom and the expanse of evergreens at the edge of the property. They were likely stuck in the cabin for at least another day given the depth of the snow and the news' warning of downed trees delaying the progress of the snow plows. And by God, if they were stuck two days before Christmas, then he intended to make the best of it. He couldn't give her the things she deserved from a man, but he could at least give her a Christmas tree.

The wind had made giant snow drifts on either side of the back door with a central path carved down the middle where the snow only came up to his ankle.

Like Moses parting the Red Sea, he thought to himself as he ventured out into the cold, a borrowed coat from the mudroom zippered against the wind and a scratchy wool hat and scarf completing the outfit. *Except God actually spoke to Moses.*

Maybe He'd talk to you if you weren't so easily distracted from your vows by the woman sleeping upstairs.

Great. Now you're hard again and picturing crawling back into bed with her.

As if you weren't already.

He tugged the hat lower on his head with one hand, the wooden handle of the ax clutched in his other, his borrowed gloves a welcome shield from the cold. The cabin was surrounded by evergreens of every size and shape, many of which would be perfect Christmas trees, but he wasn't headed for one of those paragons of yuletide. From the back door of the cabin, he'd spotted the perfect tree—thin trunk, sparse branches, shorter than the others. And if it had the added quality of being something he was fairly certain he could chop down and drag back to the cabin before Molly woke up, that was just the icing on the proverbial cake. He wanted nothing more than to delight her.

Well, he could think of a few things he wanted at least as much—to touch her again, this time in the light when he could see how beautiful she was, to warp the soft heaven between her thighs around him, to ask her to kneel for him, to touch him in return. But he wouldn't ask for those things, no matter how much he wanted to.

Lead us not into temptation...

Too late.

By the time the bottom step creaked as Molly descended, her long brown hair hanging around her shoulders and her robe tied tightly around her waist, Caleb was nearly done tightening the screws on the tree stand proudly displaying the tree. It had been harder than he expected to chop it down, and harder than that to drag it through the snow. The path from the back door to the living room was a mess of melted snow and pine needles, but he'd done it. He was struck by a wave of masculine pride, as though he'd felled a dangerous beast and not a sad-looking tree.

"What's all this?" she asked.

"I thought we could use a little Christmas spirit." He braced his hand against the tree trunk. It wobbled in its stand and he quickly pulled his hand away, willing the tree to stay upright.

"Where'd you find this...this?"

"It's a Christmas tree," he said, admiring his handywork.

Molly stifled a laugh. "That's not a Christmas tree."

"Charlie Brown would beg to differ."

"Can that thing even hold ornaments? It looks like it might droop under its own weight."

"Let's find out." He reached into the cardboard box of Christmas ornaments he'd hauled from the hall closet and pulled out a delicate green and silver glass ball, holding it out to Molly.

She plucked the ornament from his hand, her fingertips grazing his palm, and carefully hung it from one of the sturdier looking branches. Her delighted laugh sent ripples of joy through his body, a fizzy, floaty sensation coursing through his limbs. When she turned back to meet his gaze, her eyes roamed over him, stuttering on the thin black frames of his glasses.

"I didn't know you wore glasses."

He self-consciously brought his finger to the frames, adjusting them. "I don't usually. I didn't have any contact solution."

"But you had your glasses?"

"I always keep a pair in the car. I'm glad I remembered to grab them before we came in last night." The mere mention of the night before making his cock twitch with interest, and he rushed to change the subject. "I was about to make breakfast. Are you hungry?"

"I could eat."

She followed him into the kitchen, but kept a careful distance between them, as though she was giving him space to decide how this morning would go. Caleb opened the refrigerator door and stuck his head inside, hoping the cool air would calm his racing hormones. "There must be at least five packages of bacon in here."

"I wouldn't recommend cooking all five," she teased as she dropped into a chair at the small kitchen table.

"Of course not. We'll want to save at least one package for breakfast tomorrow." He took a package of bacon and the carton of eggs and set them on the counter before rifled through cabinets in search of a pan.

"You think we'll still be here tomorrow?"

He nodded as he cracked eggs into a bright purple Fiestaware bowl. "More than two feet of snow fell in the last twenty-four hours and, according to the news this morning, there are drifts of up to four feet in some places. We're lucky the power came back so quickly. I think it'll take the town all day to plow enough that we can safely get out of here. Should be clear by tomorrow morning, though." He glanced over his shoulder at her and tried to look reassuring, calm, like he wasn't such a mess of guilt and lust he couldn't even begin to worry about something as mundane as snow. "It'll be another night, but we should be back in Aster Bay by Christmas Eve."

"Is that why you put up a Christmas tree?"

He shrugged as he poured the eggs into the pan on the stove, suddenly self-conscious about his decision to drag a scraggly tree through the snow first thing in the morning.

"How did you even get it in here? Did the storm knock it down?" she asked.

"There was an ax in the hallway."

She gawked at him, her confused expression so freaking adorable he wanted to kiss it off her face.

No. Bad priest.

He leaned against the counter beside the stove and crossed his arms, unable to contain his amusement. "Did you have something you'd like to share with the class, Ms. Proulx?"

"An ax," she repeated. "Like for chopping wood."

"That is generally what tree trunks are made of, yes."

"You chopped down a tree?"

He tilted his chin towards the living room. "That tree, in fact."

"You are full of surprises." Her words hung between them, then she cleared her throat and looked away, a delicious blush creeping up her neck and onto her cheeks. He wanted to drag his tongue along her throat, see if the pretty pink color changed the way her skin tasted.

You are going to hell. Straight to hell. Do not pass go. Do not collect God's blessing.

Caleb turned back to the stove and focused on scrambling the eggs, breaking up the curds with unnecessary precision. He wanted her. Now that he knew the little noises she made when she came, how it felt to wake up with her in his arms, he knew he'd never stop wanting her. His stomach twisted, guilt and shame and something else—a whole different kind of guilt at not feeling enough shame to be able to stop.

Chapter Nine

M olly dug through the cardboard box Caleb had hauled from the closet in the hall and produced yet another crocheted snowflake. She settled it amongst the Christmas tree's sparse branches and avoided eye contact with Caleb, just as she'd done since breakfast. There'd been a moment while he was cooking when he'd looked at her and she saw something that looked an awful lot like regret flash behind his eyes.

Not that it mattered. With any luck, they'd be back on the road by the following morning and they could forget all about the temporary insanity that had gripped them the night before—insanity to think it was a good idea to cross that line with Caleb.

Insanity to think you can forget it.

Who was she kidding? She knew she'd never forget it. Just like she'd never forget the disappointment of waking up alone, or the shock of finding him in the morning beaming with pride at this scraggly tree, his hair sleep tousled, glasses perched on the bridge of his nose—the sluttiest accessory any man could wear. And that damn collar. It shouldn't make him hotter, but she didn't make the rules, and it absolutely did, even if it was the symbol of his vow to not do the very thing they'd done the night before.

But if Caleb wanted to pretend nothing happened, then that's what they would do. Even if he had gone out into the snow and chopped down a Christmas tree for her... It was probably for the best anyway.

"How did you even know where to look for Christmas ornaments?" she asked, determined to keep their conversation PG-rated.

"I took a leap of faith," he said. "Those aren't the only decorations in the closet. There's a whole box of leprechaun hats and shamrocks. And one that must be for bachelorette parties."

"Why? What's in that box?"

He hesitated, a burst of pink blooming across his cheeks and the tips of his ears. "Inflatable penises. So many inflatable penises."

She laughed, the sound pouring out of her at his beleaguered sigh. "Please tell me there were penis straws too."

"I didn't look."

"I bet you anything there are penis straws."

He pressed his lips together like he was trying not to laugh, then turned on his heel and marched into the hall. Molly continued gingerly hanging ornaments from the tree as she listened to him shuffling through boxes in the hall closet. A moment later, he returned, a shiny pink plastic penis straw sticking out of one corner of his mouth.

He grinned around the straw. "You would have won that bet."

She threw her head back and laughed. The joy of seeing Caleb like this—playful and warm and *free*—was almost overwhelming. His eyes locked on her, tracing the curve of her cheek. And was that a *twinkle* in his eye?

Come on, God. First the glasses and now a twinkle? *You're not playing fair.*

"What do I get for winning?"

"I didn't actually take the bet, so I'm pretty sure we both win."

She rolled her eyes. "Okay, fine. What do *you* get for winning?"

"This," he said, tossing aside the penis straw and handing her another ornament. "You, happy."

"Isn't that something I get?"

He shrugged. "Like I said. We both win." She turned her attention to the snowman ornament, focusing too intently on making sure it hung just right amongst the branches. It was easier when they were joking, laughing, like they'd done so many times before. Until it wasn't. Until the light shifted, highlighting the fullness of his bottom lip, the strong line of his nose, and suddenly she wasn't sure how she was going to get through another twenty-four hours without touching him again.

His heat at her back raised goosebumps at the nape of her neck. He didn't touch her, but she felt him all the same, like the space between two magnets, an invisible, tangible thing. He reached past her shoulder and hung another glass ball on the tree, moving closer, the space between them shrinking infinitesimally, but enough that she sensed it.

His voice was low when he spoke, all the earlier mirth drained away and replaced with something else. Nerves maybe. Hesitation. "I like making you happy."

She felt his words everywhere, the sandpaper rasp of them across her skin so sweet she wanted more. Molly straightened the snowman again, not that it needed it, and slowly turned towards him, though she kept her gaze on her own hands as she fidgeted with her fingers. Maybe it would be easier if they talked about it, if they looked this thing between them straight in the eyes instead of catching glimmers of what it might be.

"You already make me happy, Caleb. Last night... even if it can never happen again... I *am* happy."

He took another step towards her, his eyes dark and his brow furrowed as he studied her. Each inch he moved closer felt more ominous and more right than the last. If she extended her pinky, she'd be touching him. God, how she wanted to touch him.

"You don't look happy."

"I can be happy and sad at the same time. I contain multitudes."

He reached up and moved a strand of hair behind her ear, letting his fingertips linger on the back of her neck. Her skin sparked in its wake. "Why are you sad?"

She swallowed around the lump forming in her throat. "Because now I *know* how it could be, and I need to forget."

"I don't want you to forget." The roughness of his voice scratched at her skin. "I won't forget."

She blinked up at him, his hazel eyes so earnest. Had she misunderstood his hesitance? "Last night, I had the best dream," she said softly.

"Me too." His voice was too deep, too ragged, and it invited her to drown in it.

"I wish I was still dreaming."

He dug his fingers into her hair, tilting her face up to him as she rested her hands on his chest. He was glorious like this. Open and intriguing, and yet somehow hard, determined. Like he'd cradle her and keep her warm even as he broke her heart.

She didn't want to ask the question twisting in her gut, but she had to. "What about your vows?"

"I've already broken my vows. I break them every time I look at you. Every time I *think* about you," he said, gravel in every word.

Her chest ached at the tortured scrape of his confession, and yet it also sent that fizzy feeling racing through her blood. Like possibility. Like the calm before immeasurable pleasure. She swallowed, wetting her lips, and a strange sort of power pulsed within her when he clocked the movement.

He skated his lips over her temples, her eyelids. "Maybe this whole place is a dream."

Her fists bunched in the fabric of his shirt, holding him close, confirming for herself he was real. "We could have another day," she breathed. "Just until we go home." The thought sent off a riot of protests in her gut even as it turned her insides to fire, a mass of longing and need so potent nothing else mattered.

"I have nothing to offer you, Molly." Each word was more tormented than the last, as though this were truly the darkest of his confessions. "My life is not my own. Not yet. I want to give you everything, but—"

"I know."

She was all too aware there was no future for them, that every moment they spent even entertaining the idea of *more* was madness. But knowing didn't stop her from wanting him, even if it could only be a few stolen moments.

He backed her up, the scraggly Christmas tree shaking in its stand as she made contact with the wall. With one hand planted on the wall by her head, he ghosted the other over her curves, as though he couldn't quite bring himself to touch her yet. "We shouldn't do this."

"I know."

He gripped her hip and tugged her away from the wall, pulling her pelvis against his own before he slowly pressed them back against the wall again, his hips chasing hers. "It's a sin."

"I'm not a good Catholic anyway."

"Then I'll pray for us both." He nuzzled against her throat, dragging his lips up the long line of her neck to behind her ear. "Tell me to stop, Molly."

"No." She tugged him closer and tilted her head to give him better access to her throat. If he stopped now, she'd combust on the spot.

A low, menacing sound rumbled in Caleb's chest as he drew her earlobe between his teeth, nipping at the sensitive skin. "Tell. Me. To. Stop."

She hooked her index finger over the top of his collar and tugged the piece of white plastic free. It fell to the floor at their feet. "I don't want you to stop, Father."

Chapter Ten

Caleb's brain turned to static at Molly's use of his title, the depravity of it coiling within him, pulling tighter and tighter until he was practically shaking with need. Would giving them both this moment, just for a little while, really be so much worse than what he'd already done? Would God forgive him any less?

Her amber eyes gleamed at him in anticipation and, for the first time in months, he wanted to pray. Not to confess or ask for forgiveness, though Lord knew he needed both, but a prayer of gratitude that this woman had crossed his path, that she wanted him as much as he wanted her, that he got to be the man to see her like this. He tightened his hold on her hair, tugging gently, and her pupils widened, darkened, naked hunger dancing across her face. How could he ask for forgiveness when he wasn't even a little bit sorry?

"Say it again," he commanded.

She licked her lips, eyes dancing between his. "Don't stop, Father."

Caleb crashed his mouth against hers, kissing the name off her lips as though he could taste the broken vow if he kissed her hard enough. It tasted sweeter than his twenty-five years of self-restraint ever could have imagined. She licked into his mouth, urging him closer with her hands in his hair. Desperate and deep, like she'd devour him if he didn't devour her first.

Had kissing always been like this? No, it couldn't have been, or he'd never have been able to go so long without it. This wasn't just kissing—it was like breathing, like drowning. How had he not known it could be like this?

And how could he ever be expected to give it up again now that he knew?

His hands tightened in her hair and he slid his thigh between her legs, just as he'd done the night before. A damp heat soaked through the fabric where she moved against the hard muscle of his thigh and his cock kicked behind the placket of his pants at the idea of sinking into that heat. Panting, he pulled away, slamming his hand into the wall beside her head, and used his other hand to undo the belt of her robe. Despite his shaking hand, the robe fell open easily.

"Ms. Proulx, where is your underwear?" He heard the darkness in his tone, but it only seemed to spur her on. He wrapped a hand around her hip and guided her movements, urging her to grind against him harder, all the while transfixed by the sight of her riding his thigh. "You've been down here all morning with a bare pussy."

She gasped at his use of the filthy word, her eyes going liquid, and he wondered what else he could say to put that glazed look of impending pleasure on her face.

"You like when I say dirty things to you, angel?"

"Yes," she panted, steadying herself with hands planted on his shoulders.

"You're so wet already. You're soaking me, Molly."

She arched an eyebrow. "Did you want me to apologize for that?"

"Don't you dare." He slid his hand down over the curve of her belly and gripped the top of her thigh, his thumb brushing the short curls covering her mound. With his free hand, he pushed the robe off her shoulders, the terrycloth pooling at their feet. Her breasts moved in mesmerizing ways as she rode his thigh, her dusky pink nipples pulled into tight, puckered points. "You are so beautiful," he whispered, trailing his fingers along the outer edge of her breast. He curled his hand around her ribcage, using his hold to raise the full curve as he bent to brush his lips over her nipple.

"Caleb," she groaned.

She dug her fingernails into his bicep and he lifted his thigh a fraction of an inch higher. The little moan she loosed in response was like a fist closing around his throat. Dangerous. A warning. And yet he wanted more.

"Do you think you can come like this, with nothing but my thigh between yours?"

"I don't know," she half sobbed, grinding against him harder in her search for release.

He bit down gently on her nipple and she sucked in a shocked breath, her hips moving faster. "I think you can." A flick of his tongue to soothe the bite. "Have faith."

She half laughed at his teasing reproach, but the sound dissolved into another moan. "I need..." She broke off on a frustrated sound.

"I know." He pressed back against her movements, urging her on with the hand gripping her thigh. "Come for me like this. Let me watch your pretty pussy soak my thigh, and then I'll give you what you need, angel."

Her eyes fell closed as her orgasm hit, and he wasn't sure where to look first. His eyes darted from the contraction of her stomach muscles to the tempting quiver of her thighs, from the wetness spreading over the fabric of his slacks to the hypnotic bounce of her full breasts, from the pure bliss on her face to lips parted as if surprised by her own pleasure. He dropped her breast and threaded his fingers through her own, pressing their hands against the wall above her head as he kissed her, drinking the little gasps from her lips.

With each quiver, each moan, each half-moon sting of her fingernails on his bicep, he knew he was ruined. As her frenzy subsided, he lowered his leg, moving it from between her thighs despite the sound of protest bubbling up from her throat. He chuckled, delighted by her open desire even as he was undone by it.

She opened her eyes, bright, liquid heat focused on him as she loosened her grip on his arm and dragged her hand down his chest. She hooked a finger through the belt loop at his waist and tugged gently.

Her intention was clear, but he couldn't take off his pants now. If she touched him now, with that look in her eyes and the proof of her pleasure coating his thigh, he'd embarrass himself. He needed a minute to collect himself, and even then... It had been more than two decades since he'd been with a woman. He was likely to come too quickly. But not yet. He wasn't ready for this to be over yet.

Caleb tilted his chin towards the rug in front of the fireplace. "Lie down."

She seemed to want to protest, but at the last minute changed her mind. He watched as she moved to the rug, all soft skin and plush curves, each step making her thighs jiggle, her belly, her breasts, like her body had been designed to draw his attention even in something as simple as walking. She lay back on the rug, propping herself up on her elbows but keeping her knees closed, hiding the most intimate part of herself from him. And that wouldn't do.

The glow of the flames in the fireplace licked across her creamy skin, pink and golden light dancing along her silhouette, beckoning him closer. He dropped to his knees in front of her and slowly unbuttoned his shirt, shedding the clerical black while he held her gaze. She only broke eye contact once, when his shirt fell from his shoulders and she made a slow perusal of his naked chest, heat sparking behind her eyes. He pressed the heel of his hand against his aching cock through his pants, determined to stave off his own need as long as possible, but when she looked at him like that, something primal roared to life beneath his skin, demanding he fuck her now, claim her, make her his.

"You have to stop looking at me like that."

Her lips quirked up at the corner and she arched her eyebrow. "How am I looking at you?"

"Like you've thought about this as much as I have." Her mouth pulled into a shocked little O. What he wouldn't give to push into the perfect O of her lips. But not yet. Not yet. "Open your legs, Molly."

She dropped her knees to the side, revealing herself to him once more, her obedience thrilling. He lowered himself to his belly between her thighs, resting on his elbows so he could get a closer look. The heady scent of her arousal curled around his nostrils, urging him on. Using his thumbs, he parted her, cataloging the needy flutter of her most secret place, the moisture gathered at her entrance. Glancing up, he met her eyes, an intrigued look in them as she watched him examine her. Her chest rose and fell with each breath, her nipples impossibly hard and cheeks flushed.

"Lay back, angel. Let me worship you."

She drew her bottom lip between her teeth as she followed his command. Her compliance, her trust, sent fresh jolts of electricity racing down his spine and he nuzzled against her mound, breathing in her scent, his lips a hairsbreadth away from the glistening bud of her clit.

How could this woman be so perfectly made that her need should call to his own? How could he have the power to bring her satisfaction, and be expected *not* to worship her?

He flattened his tongue and dragged it over her clit in a long, unhurried stroke. He worked slowly, experimenting with speed and pressure, noting the way she bucked her hips when he pressed the point of his tongue in just the right spot, the way her breathing sped up when he sucked on the swollen bud. When she began to tremble beneath him, her body seemingly unable to decide if she wanted to press against him harder or pull back, he wound his arms under her thighs and pulled her tight to his mouth, keeping her locked against him.

Her clit pulsed beneath his tongue as he drew each moan and gasp from her, the sweetness of her arousal coating his lips and chin in his relentless pursuit of her pleasure. And when at last she cried out, arching her back, her hips moving mindlessly against his mouth, he thanked God for the gift of her taste on his tongue.

Molly could hardly catch her breath, the aftershocks of her second orgasm rippling through her with each new kiss Caleb dropped against her overheated skin. He blew a stream of cool air against her clit and she groaned, shuddering when he pressed another too gentle kiss to the sensitive spot. His stubbled jaw scraped pleasantly against her thighs in stark contrast to the softness of his kiss.

"Caleb," she groaned, tugging on his hair, "kiss me."

"I am kissing you." She could hear the smirk in his voice.

"You know what I meant."

"You like when I kiss you here." Another too soft press of his lips, a flick of his tongue sending a bolt of pleasure through her.

"Father West," she said in her best teacher voice.

He froze and for a moment she wondered if it had been the wrong thing to say, but when he looked up at her from between her thighs, his pupils were blown black, ringed by a thin circle of green. "That is not the way to get me to stop kissing your pussy, Ms. Proulx," he warned.

Another tug on his hair and his eyes narrowed.

"I want to kiss you too," she said.

With one last forlorn glance between her legs, he crawled over her body, settling his hips between hers and balancing his weight on his palms by her shoulders. The starchy fabric of his pants was rough against the skin of her inner thighs, but she wrapped her legs around him all the same, pulling him closer so she could press her lips to his. He tasted like her, and suddenly she was met with a fresh wave of heat arrowing down to her core. She trailed her nails down his chest, cataloging the little grunt of pleasure he made in response, and hooked her fingers through his belt loops.

She tugged. "I want to kiss you here."

He lifted his face enough to meet her eyes, searching, as though he expected to find she was lying. As if she hadn't been fantasizing about his cock for months. She palmed the impressive bulge in his pants, biting back a smile when he groaned in response.

"Please, Caleb. Let me touch you."

He rolled off of her and for a moment she thought he was going to tell her no, that he was going to put an end to it right then and there. Instead, he sat up on his knees and, as he held her gaze, slowly worked his belt open. The metal buckle clattered against the hardwood floor as he tossed the belt aside. He waited, an invitation and an out all in one. But Molly didn't want an out. She wanted him, every messy moment she could grasp hold of before time ran out.

She scrambled to her knees in front of him and drew down his zipper, shoving his pants and boxer briefs down around his thighs. His cock bobbed between them, long and thick and ready for her. The flared red tip leaked precum, glistening as it dripped down the length of his erection. She wrapped her hand around him, squeezing at the base. When she began pumping over him in slow, tight strokes, he hissed and fell back to sitting, his back resting against the couch, as though staying upright while she touched him was too challenging.

Molly knelt by his side, scooting closer until her knees brushed his thighs, and continued to slowly stroke him. "Come here," he said, his voice gruff, as he grasped her hip and pulled her even closer. He caressed her backside, taking great handfuls of her ass, before sliding his hand between her legs again, dipping his fingers inside. "You're so soft," he marveled.

"You're so hard," she teased.

"Perfect opposites."

"Just perfect." She leaned forward and wrapped her lips around the head of his cock, taking only the tip into her mouth. His fingers stilled between her legs, as if his entire body had frozen when her lips made contact with his erection, before he redoubled his efforts, pumping harder, deeper.

"You're perfect," he said.

"Shh." She flicked her tongue over the ridge at his crown. "It's my turn to worship you."

She lowered her mouth over him, taking him as deep as she could—which, given his impressive length and girth, wasn't very deep. All the same, he sucked in a breath as though he'd been punched in the chest.

"That's blasphemy, Ms. Proulx," he choked out.

She did it again, dragging the flat of her tongue over the underside of his erection as she moved up and down, up and down. He pressed his thumb to her clit, working her in the tight circles she liked, and her climax coiled low in her belly, tighter and tighter with each of his movements.

"Molly," he said through gritted teeth, "I'm not going to last long." She hummed around him, and he cursed under his breath, his head falling back. "Come for me, Molly. Come with me."

She rocked back against his fingers, driving them deeper into the place behind her clit that made her see stars, while she continued to suck his cock. He said her name again, a pained, tense warning, and then, just as she fell over into yet another climax, he gripped her hair with his free hand and pulled her off his cock. Thick ropes of cum spurted from the tip and lashed across her breasts. She rode his hand, her inner muscles clenching around his fingers, as he coated her in his release. It felt like being anointed, baptized even, like the start of something new, something that would fundamentally change them both.

When at last they'd both finished, he withdrew his fingers, pressing each one inside his mouth and sucking them clean, his eyes locked on hers with such intensity she thought she might burst into flame. She watched as he used that same hand to massage his cum into her skin, spreading it over her breasts, circling her nipples in deliberate strokes.

"How are you even more beautiful now than you've ever been?" he whispered.

"That's just the orgasm talking."

He pinched her nipple, twisting until she gasped at the sharp bite of pain before releasing her. "No, it's not."

They sat together in silence, idly touching each other, his fingertips dancing over her belly, her breasts, her hand resting on his thigh. Easy. The way it would be if this thing between them could be more than a snowed-in fever dream. The casual caresses and quiet care that underscored a life together.

But this wasn't that. And as her body cooled, doubt began to creep in. She drew her knees up to her chest, wrapping her arms around them. Though he let his hand fall away, he frowned at the change in her position.

"Don't shut me out, Molly."

"I'm not."

He shot her a disbelieving look, but the doubt had well and truly caught hold of her now, twisting in her stomach and crawling up her throat. "Tell me what you're thinking," he said, command slipping into his voice and making her want to curl up at his side and do whatever he asked.

She shook her head, as though she could shake free the voice at the back of her brain telling her to stop this now. Every second she let this continue would only make it hurt more when it ended. "I was thinking, we should make gingerbread cookies."

He eyed her warily. "Gingerbread?"

"Mmhmm." She forced brightness into her voice she didn't feel. "If we only have twenty-four hours, then we should do it all. Make all the Christmas memories."

He slid his hands into her hair and held her captive so she had to meet his eyes, a spark twinkling behind his eyes despite his stern expression and the careful way he studied her, as though he were looking for a crack in her story, an indication she didn't mean it. "And what other memories did you want to make, Ms. Proulx?"

"We could start with a shower," she said, glancing down at her chest.

He bit back a smile and pressed a kiss to her lips, chaste and lingering. "A shower sounds perfect."

Chapter Eleven

"If we're going to make gingerbread today, we better get started. The dough needs time to chill before we can roll it out." Molly gave her hair one last scrunch with the towel, then tossed it aside and led the way downstairs, Caleb close on her heels. Her hips moved in enticing ways as she descended the stairs, and he knew, beneath her jeans, she was bare, her underwear from the day before left behind in her room. How was a man supposed to focus on baking when Molly Proulx was going commando?

"I didn't realize it was such a process."

"Still want to make it?"

"Obviously."

In the kitchen, Molly rifled through the cabinets, pulling out small spice jars and giant bags of flour and brown sugar. "Are you good at math?" she asked as she set a stick of butter on the counter to soften.

"I'm alright. Why?"

"Tessa's recipe makes something like eight dozen cookies. We're going to need to cut it down to a quarter of the size at least." She rose up on her tip toes and reached for a jar of molasses at the back of the cabinet.

Caleb gripped her hip and pressed her back to his front, reaching past her and pulling down the jar with ease. He set it on the counter, but didn't move away, a warm sort of satisfaction he hadn't experienced before washing over him when she leaned back against his chest.

"I thought your mom taught you to make gingerbread."

"She did, but I don't have the recipe memorized. I texted Tessa this morning while you were chopping down that sickly-looking tree."

"Hey, you leave my tree out of it," he said, but he couldn't stop grinning.

She suppressed a smile and tilted her head towards the pile of X-rated gingerbread men cookie cutters they'd collected from the upstairs hall nativity scene and relocated to the kitchen counter. "I could hardly have these cookie cutters staring us in the face and not use them."

He pulled the oversized red Fiestaware mixing bowl down from its perch on top of the refrigerator, far out of Molly's reach. Their hands brushed as she took the bowl from him, sending awareness skittering across his skin.

Ridiculous. You spent the better part of an hour with your tongue between her legs and you're getting worked up over touching her hand.

Her eyes slid over him, across his shoulders and down his biceps to where he'd rolled up the sleeves of his shirt, as though she could hear his dirty thoughts. Or maybe she was just having dirty thoughts of her own. As her gaze hit the bare skin of his forearms, need pulsed through her blood and pulled the bowl towards herself, positioning it like a barrier between them. "Of course, Tessa did try to convince me to make snickerdoodles instead."

He watched as she carefully measured the fragrant spices out into the mixing bowl. "I was never a big snickerdoodle fan. The name always makes me think of dogs. Poodles. Labradoodles. Snickerdoodles. They sound too much alike."

She laughed and pointed to the stand mixer on the counter. "Make yourself useful and start beating the butter."

He waggled his eyebrows at her. "I feel like there's an innuendo there I can't quite put my finger on."

"You put your finger on plenty already."

"And here I thought we were just getting started."

He captured her around the waist, tugging her against him and dropping a kiss on her lips. How was he supposed to stop touching her? For the first time, he understood why his brother and their friends were so obnoxious about being publicly affectionate with their wives and girlfriends.

She stepped out of the circle of his arms, her smile infectious as she straightened his glasses. "Pace yourself, Father."

He sighed dramatically but released her all the same. Molly moved about the kitchen with ease, measuring flour and cracking eggs into her assembled bowls. He was so busy watching her, he almost forgot to turn on the stand mixer.

This is what it would be like. The idea rushed through him like the wind, kicking up all the long-discarded thoughts he'd tried to ignore. Thoughts that had coalesced into the shape of a curvy English teacher. Thoughts he knew would not be so easily discarded a second time around.

You could be laicized. You could walk away.

The first time he'd considered leaving the priesthood was shortly after his ordination. He'd woken one night in a cold sweat, panic gripping his throat at the idea of a life alone with this taciturn God who so often withheld his voice. But Father Raymond had convinced him to see it through, to trust the Church to guide him. To trust God. Twenty-five years on, his trust in God hadn't wavered. He couldn't say the same for his faith in the Church.

He thought of the laicization paperwork sitting in his email, of the Bishop's offer to reassign him instead.

Maybe God put you here to show you a new path.

"If you were in Aster Bay today, what would you be doing?"

The question pulled his focus back to the task at hand. The butter was well and truly beaten, and he shut off the stand mixer, leaning against the counter as he watched her work. "I was supposed to be helping Ethan and the guys get ready for the toy drive. The parents pick up this afternoon. What about you?"

She hummed as she thought, her hips swaying to a tune only she could hear as she stirred the sweet concoction in her bowl. "Jo would probably rope me into going Christmas shopping with her. She always saves it until the last minute."

"Unlike you."

She glanced up at him, her lips tipped up in a soft smile. He wanted to press his tongue into the dimple that appeared in her cheek. "I was done with my shopping before Thanksgiving," she confirmed.

"I knew it."

"And then I would probably spend the evening reading the draft of Alex Lambert's college scholarship essay." She paused for a moment, twisting her lips up to the side and glancing around for her phone. "I need to let him know I won't get to it until after Christmas."

"Will that be okay? He won't miss his deadline, will he?"

She scoffed. "No. Even if I didn't finish reading his essay until after New Year's, he'd still be more than a month ahead of the deadline. That boy doesn't miss deadlines."

"He's a good kid." A bolt of pain gathered behind Caleb's eyes as their earlier conversation about the St. Anthony's High senior came back to him. He scraped his hand over his jaw. "Will it affect his chances if he doesn't make valedictorian?"

Molly's shoulders stiffened, but she shrugged, avoiding his eyes as she combined the wet and dry ingredients. "It might."

"I'll talk to Bruce when we get back." Her brow furrowed as though she wasn't quite sure if she believed him. "He can't mess up a kid's future over a uniform violation."

She rolled her bottom lip through her teeth and nodded slowly, turning her attention back to her baking, but the air between them soured, as though they were vibrating at different frequencies.

"What aren't you saying?"

She sighed, using the back of her hand to push her hair out of her face as she turned back to him. "It's not about the uniform violation, and it's not just this kid."

"I know."

"Do you? Bruce Day is waging war on every student who dares to be anything other than a model Catholic, and he believes he has the full support of the Church. *That* is the issue you need to address with him. Not the uniform violation."

His headache intensified, like there were strings behind his eyes slowly being pulled tighter and tighter. "It's a Catholic school, Molly. He does have the support of the Church."

She pressed her lips together and nodded tightly. When she made to turn away again, he caught her around the waist, stopping her mid spin. She wouldn't meet his eyes, so he bent his knees, looking up at her through his eyelashes. "But he doesn't have *my* support. And I will let him know I do not believe he has God's either."

Her eyes flashed to his. "He won't believe you."

"He's entitled to his own relationship with God. And so are those kids, no matter what he thinks the Church says."

"How can you stand it? How can you believe the teachings are wrong and perpetuate them anyway?"

"Both can be true. The Church can be flawed and also be worth preserving."

"When too much of the foundation is rotten, you don't try to preserve the house. You knock the whole damn thing down and build something new."

He dug his hand into his hair, tugging at the ends. "What are you talking about?"

"It's a metaphor. How much of the Church needs to be flawed before it's no longer worth perpetuating its teachings? How many rotten boards can be a part of the frame before you're better off starting fresh?"

He pinched the bridge of his nose, trying to keep up with her metaphors. "You want me to start a new religion?"

"No. I'm just trying to understand where your tipping point is. How much of the religion you preach must be antithetical to your own beliefs before you're no longer willing to align yourself with it?"

He blinked at her, the question reverberating through his bones, drawing the fraying threads of his convictions to the surface, doubt and shame winding around his limbs and binding him in a never-ending battle between his intentions and his reality. "I'm not the only one aligning myself with the Church. Last time I checked, you work for it too."

Something like disbelief flashed across her face. "I work for the school."

"You're splitting hairs."

Anger flickered in her eyes. "Maybe I won't for much longer."

"What does that mean?" She pressed her lips together, clearly not willing to elaborate. "What am I supposed to do, Molly? It's been twenty-five years. This is all I know."

"But it's not all you are!"

He hung his head and huffed out a breath. She slipped her hand into his, palm to palm, fingers lacing together as though she could knit together those fraying threads with their interlocked hands.

"You do so much good, Caleb. You help so many of the kids you set out to reach when you joined the priesthood. Sometimes I wonder..."

"What?"

"How many more could you reach if you weren't required to put yourself in opposition to the Church to do so?"

"If I weren't a priest, you mean." He'd never said the words out loud before to anyone but his confessor and the Bishop, given voice to the fragile wisp of an idea flickering in the darkest recesses of his heart.

She dropped his hand. The loss of her touch stung. "I'm just trying to understand," she repeated, her voice small.

"So am I."

"You said God sent you a sign when you were in college and so you became a priest. But what about the other signs he's been sending you?"

"God hasn't spoken to me in years," he said, unable to contain the bitterness in his voice.

She cocked her head to the side, brows drawn together. "Maybe you're just not listening."

"I'm trying! I keep asking for a sign, for something—anything—to show me the path forward. And nothing!"

He scrubbed his hand over his hair, the ache in his chest yawning open as he swallowed the rest of it. He didn't deserve a sign from God, not when he was actively breaking his vows again and again. Not when he was desperate to end this conversation, not just because he wanted to stuff these feelings back into the little box at the back of his heart, but also because he wanted to kiss her again, to go back to the dream world they'd been living in.

"I've given my life to Him and it's still not enough." Though whether he meant it wasn't enough for himself or for God he wasn't sure.

She exhaled slowly, smoothing her flour-dusted palms over his chest. "You are a very good priest."

"Not so good," he said, pressing his mouth to her temple just to feel the warmth of her skin against his lips.

She smiled, though it didn't quite meet her eyes. "I'm sorry."

"Me too."

"I didn't mean... You are not responsible for the faults of your religion."

He considered her statement, rolling it around his mind. It wasn't quite right, but he couldn't figure out why. "Religion is not the same thing as faith, and I know you may not believe this, but I'm not interested in perpetuating the religion. I have only ever been interested in the faith."

"And yet you work for the religion."

"I do," he conceded.

But what if he didn't? What if he chose a different life?

Please, God, send me a sign.

Chapter Twelve

"That is not a Christmas movie." Molly wrestled the remote control out of Caleb's hands and continued scrolling through the options on the screen mounted above the fireplace. She struggled to contain her laughter at the incredulous look he shot her from his spot on the couch beside her.

"But *Moonstruck* is?"

"Absolutely."

Caleb hooked her knees with his arm and pulled her legs over his lap, settling one hand on her calf and reaching for another gingerbread cookie with his other. Their clothing had finally finished washing and drying after their morning activities under the Christmas tree, but he almost wished they'd forgotten to make use of the appliances in the upstairs hall closet. He'd much rather have her bare legs across his lap than be separated from her by her jeans and his black dress pants. At least he'd left his collar in its place on his nightstand.

He squeezed her calf, tracing the seam of her jeans with his thumb and bit off the head of a particularly obscene gingerbread man. "Bruce Willis literally wears a Santa hat."

"*Die Hard* is not a Christmas movie. It is a movie set at Christmas. That's different."

"How is that different from *Moonstruck*?" he asked around a bite of gingerbread.

"*Moonstruck* is cozy."

"Infidelity and missing limbs are cozy?"

"I don't make the rules. Ooh! What about *While You Were Sleeping*?"

"Isn't that the one where she's supposed to be engaged to one guy but she falls in love with his brother?"

"Yes, but it's complicated. And romantic."

"What is with you and movies where the heroine falls in love with her fiancé's brother?" He tickled her side just so she would squirm in his lap. "Do I need to be worried here, Ms. Proulx?"

"Last I checked, you weren't my fiancé, Father West."

He knew she'd meant it as a joke, but the words stung all the same. It wasn't that she'd said he wasn't her fiancé—that was objectively true. It was the other truth, the implicit understanding he would *never* be her fiancé.

He loved this little bubble they were in, but it was littered with landmines. How was he meant to navigate this in between where they kissed and touched and acted like a couple and also keep himself from wanting all the things he'd vowed never to have? When they returned to Aster Bay in the morning, he would go back to being a priest and she would go back to being the schoolteacher he couldn't stop thinking about. He'd always known that was the only way this could end, so why did the reminder sour in his stomach?

Molly leaned forward and cupped his jaw with her palm. "I'm sorry. It was a stupid joke."

"Except it's not a joke. I'm not your fiancé. I'm not your anything."

Determination sparked in her eyes and she scratched lightly at his stubble with her nails. "Right now, you are. Here, you are."

His hand curled around her ankle, his thumb gliding over her skin in slow strokes. Here and now. That's all they had promised to each other, all he could offer, a brief intermission from real life. He'd spend the rest of his days trying to learn how to atone for a sin he couldn't regret. They hadn't taught him what kind of penance to assign for that during his formation.

"How about *Elf*?" she asked. "No brothers involved."

He nodded, allowing her to navigate the conversation back to safer territory. As she selected the movie he tugged her against his side, tucking her head beneath his chin. "I'm pretty sure there's a brother in *Elf*."

"Half-brother. And he's a child. Doesn't count."

His lips brushed against her hair, and he breathed in her scent. "You have a lot of rules for Christmas movies."

"Shhh. It's starting."

She snuggled against his chest. If he hadn't known such a thing was biologically impossible, he would have sworn his heart grew three sizes, just like the Grinch she'd once claimed to be. He hardly watched the movie, reveling in the weight of her curled against him, legs draped over his lap, hands and face on his chest, the tips of her middle and index fingers slipping through the holes between the buttons on his shirt. He wanted her there always, warm and sleepy, a tangle of limbs.

He kissed her forehead and she tilted her chin up to him, a small, secret smile on her lips. A smile just for him. She pressed that smile against his mouth, a quick brush of lips before she turned back to the movie, as he struggled to place the emotion suffusing every part of him.

Happiness, yes, but not only that. Or maybe it was more about what he *wasn't* feeling—doubt, shame. Somehow their absence was so much louder than the emotions themselves had been when they howled in his chest. Because how could he doubt he was meant to hold this woman? How could he be ashamed of caring for her, of—

Careful, Caleb.

It took Molly exactly thirty-seven minutes to fall asleep curled up in his lap, her cheek resting against his heart. Thirty-seven minutes for him to picture what life could be like—the little condo they would rent near his brother's house in Aster Bay so they could be close to family and friends, the evening walks through town to get ice cream, the way he'd hold her hand as they strolled the farmers' market. Falling asleep in her arms, reaching for her in the night, making love to her for the rest of his days. Her belly growing round with his child, the family they could build...

She nuzzled closer, rubbing her cheek and nose against his chest like a contented kitten. They'd both need new jobs. He would never be welcome in a Catholic church again and she wouldn't be able to keep working at St. Anthony's, not after having an affair with a disgraced priest. Then there were the townspeople—his parishioners, most likely—who would talk...

But you'd have her.

In his pocket, his phone dinged and he moved to retrieve it without jostling her too much. The dings continued rapid fire, as his brother and their friends shot off message after message in the group chat.

> **Gavin:** How're you guys holding up? Haven't heard from you in a while.
>
> **Jamie:** They're fine. It's just Maine.
>
> **Gavin:** They're snowed in!
>
> **Baz:** In a massive cabin.
>
> **Ethan:** Jo told Hannah she heard from Molly

this morning.

Gavin: Send proof of life!

He grinned to himself and held out his phone, angling the camera carefully to make sure none of Molly's hair was in the frame, the tips of her fingers just beyond the edge of the image. He snapped a shot and sent it back.

Caleb: We're fine. Watching Christmas movies. Hopefully we'll be headed home tomorrow.

Baz: Where's your collar?

Shit. He traced the space at the base of his throat where his clerical collar usually sat, but his fingers only met bare skin. How could he have been so careless to forget he wasn't wearing it before he sent that picture?

Ethan: You won't even take that thing off for family dinner, but you take it off to watch a movie?

Caleb: It's not a big deal. I'm allowed to take it off.

Jamie: But you never do.

There are a lot of things I never do that I've done in the last twenty-four hours.

His phone burst to life, vibrating and ringing in his grip, the sound far too loud. On his chest, Molly stirred and grumbled little noises of protest against his shirt. He fumbled to turn down the volume, pressing buttons too quickly, too haphazardly. The screen lit up, his brother's concerned face filling the screen.

"Shit," Caleb swore, the phone slipping in his grasp as his own image filled the box in the corner of the screen—an image that included a clear shot of Molly sleeping in his lap.

"What's going on? Is that Molly?" Gavin asked, his eyes going wide.

Caleb panicked, hanging up the call just before he dropped his phone. It landed with a thud on Molly's knee.

She groaned, lifting her face up to his. "Why is your phone attacking me?"

In her lap, the phone started ringing again. Caleb snatched it up and got to his feet, unceremoniously dislodging her in the process as he bolted from the room, taking the stairs two at a time and shouting an apology over his shoulder as he went. He didn't answer the call until he was safely behind the door of his bedroom—not that he'd slept in it the night before.

Shit!

"What's going on?" Gavin asked again when Caleb answered.

"Nothing."

"Why are you out of breath? And why aren't you wearing your collar?"

"It's not—You're making a big deal out of nothing."

"Am I? Why was Molly in your lap?"

"She—"

"Lying is a sin, Father West." Gavin arched an expectant eyebrow at his brother through the phone.

Caleb scraped his hand over his face as he took a seat on the edge of his bed. "You're a pain in the ass, you know that?"

"I do, in fact. Now tell me what's going on."

He shook his head, glancing away. "You're not my confessor."

"No, I'm your brother. And you're avoiding the question." When he didn't answer, Gavin released a long-suffering sigh. "Did you *lose* your collar?"

"Of course not." Caleb grabbed the plastic tab off his nightstand and held it up for the camera.

"Why are you so defensive? Caleb—" Gavin's forehead wrinkled, his eyes flashing with a curiosity that reminded Caleb of days spent trying to figure out what creature was eating all the sugar snap peas growing in their mother's backyard, the determined interest with which his little brother would stake out the raised beds for hours on end in hopes of catching a glimpse of the culprit. "You look different."

Caleb blanched. "You're imagining things."

"I don't think so."

With a frustrated harumph, Caleb slid the tabs of the clerical collar into place. "There? Is that better?" The collar chafed, the rigid plastic too restrictive, suffocating, even without buttoning the top button of his shirt.

"Worse." The curiosity in Gavin's eyes melted into something like hurt. "It's just me, man. What's going on?"

Caleb tore the collar from his throat and tossed it on the bed beside him. He lowered his voice. "I fucked up." But that wasn't quite right... "I made a mess of things." *Try again.* "I—"

His voice broke and he glanced away, eyes zeroing in on that simple collar against the blue and yellow quilt. *The truth will set you free.*

"I think I'm falling in love with Molly."

"I mean...yeah, Caleb. Are you just figuring that out now?"

Caleb snapped his eyes back to his brother's sympathetic face on the screen, his own surprise at Gavin's reaction staring back at him.

"It's been pretty damn obvious for a while. But you're...you know," Gavin said, gesturing towards Caleb.

"I know," he said miserably.

"Is this the first time you've had feelings for someone since becoming a priest?"

"Yes! It's not exactly something we're encouraged to do."

"Right, but it's just a feeling. You can't control how you feel." Caleb's face heated as his cheeks turned bright red on the screen. Gavin's eyes grew wide. "Unless, it's more than just a feeling?"

"I slept with her." Gavin's eyes nearly popped out of his head. "I mean, I didn't—technically, yes, we slept together but we didn't *sleep together*, and then this morning, that wasn't sleeping but—"

Gavin held up a hand to stop Caleb's ramblings. "I'm sorry. I'm having trouble following here. Did you share a bed with her, or did you have sex?"

"Yes? I mean, I'm not sure exactly what qualifies as sex in this particular circumstance—"

"Did either one of you come?" Caleb glared at his brother, as if there was any world in which he was answering that question. Gavin blew out a breath. "Okay, so you had sex with her. Didn't you...I mean, isn't that against the rules?"

"Yes!" Caleb leapt to his feet and paced the length of the small room, his bare toes digging into the low pile of the carpet. "This whole thing is against the rules. This is exactly why I should let the Bishop transfer me."

"You *what*?"

"It's not important."

"I think it is fucking important, thank you very much," Gavin snapped. "Since when do you not tell me things like that?"

"Like what?"

"Like major life things! Like you're thinking about leaving Aster Bay again. Like falling in love with my wife's best friend. Like breaking your vows—"

"I just told you!"

Caleb ran a hand through his hair, adjusted his glasses, and sank back down onto the bed. The weight of his decisions over the last twenty-four hours slammed into him like a wrecking ball, shattering bone and bruising skin. It was painful and awful and yet somehow also liberating, like he'd been encased in amber and had finally broken free.

"And so you took off your collar because—"

"Actually, she took it off."

The brothers stared at each other for a moment in stunned silence before they both chuckled, Caleb's need to correct Gavin on that particular detail only serving to highlight the absurdity of the entire situation.

"Merry Christmas, Father West," Gavin teased as only a little brother could. "She's one step away from jingling your bells."

"Don't be gross," Caleb chided.

"So what are you going to do now?"

Caleb cast his eyes around the room as though the solution to his existential crisis somehow lay within the four walls of his rented bedroom. "I don't know."

"What do you want to do?"

"I want to be with her," he admitted, then just as quickly he wrote over the confession. "I want to go back in time twenty-four hours and never have gotten into this mess. I want to go back twenty-five years— I took a vow."

On the screen, Gavin frowned. "Did I ever tell you what Mom said to me the night you told us you were going to become a priest?"

"No, I don't think so."

"You'd just come home from college for summer break and we went out for burgers at the Dockside Diner."

"I remember."

"And then you dropped this bomb on us. Mom asked you why. Do you remember what you told her?"

"I told her I wanted to help people."

Gavin nodded. "And she said you could help people by becoming a therapist or a guidance counselor or a social worker."

He frowned as he tried to remember that part of the conversation. "I don't remember that."

"You kept rattling on about how you'd met this priest in school and it was a sign from God or Dad or whoever and now you were going to be a priest too. You barely heard a word she said and then you left dinner early to go to evening Mass at St. Anthony's. As soon as you left the diner, Mom turned to me and said you were lost."

"Lost?"

"She said you'd been lost for years, searching for something or someone to tell you which way to go and what to do, and she supposed if you had to find someone to listen to, there were worse people than a priest. But she hoped you weren't going to end up even more lost than before."

Caleb swallowed hard, recalling a similar conversation with his mother on the night before he took his vows. "Meeting Father Raymond, the life he offered me, it *was* a sign," he said slowly, resolutely. "I believe that."

"Maybe it was. But, Caleb, what about all the other signs you've been getting?"

"What signs?" he scoffed. "God doesn't send me signs anymore. He doesn't—" He broke off, shaking his head.

"What kind of priest am I when He doesn't even talk to me anymore?"

"Maybe that's your sign."

"The absence of a sign isn't a sign."

"There's no such thing as signs!" Gavin's frustration bubbled over, his free hand gesticulating as he spoke. "There have never been any signs. It's all just choices! God didn't tell you to become a priest, just like Dad didn't tell you to become a priest. You told yourself that because it was the choice that felt right."

"But that feeling *is* the sign," he argued.

"Then what about the feelings you're having now? Why are they any less of a sign than the one you had in college?" Caleb didn't have an answer for that. "Call it whatever you want—signs, intuition, whatever. It's all the same thing at the end of the day. It's the information available to you at the time and the choices you make. Right now, the information in front of you is you have feelings for Molly—big feelings. Big enough feelings to give in to your pants feelings. And she feels the same way about you. So what are you going to do about it?"

He dragged his knuckles over his eyes behind his glasses. "I don't know how to make that choice, Gav. I'm not free to make it."

"Then get yourself free. But if you're waiting for some *sign* to give you permission to be happy..." Gavin shook his head. "My wife was literally cast opposite me on a dating show and I still tried to tell myself I wasn't supposed to love her."

"Look how well that worked out," Caleb said with a half-hearted smile.

"She's my wife now, isn't she? I'd say it worked out fan-fucking-tastically. What's that story about God sending help to the man in the flood? From what I can tell from your texts, you and Molly were literally sent a star to follow, a stable to sleep in, and a snowstorm to force you to face how you feel."

"I want to." Caleb's voice was small, almost as though he was afraid to admit the truth even to himself. "I love her." The words grew in his chest, warm and glowing as they took root behind his rib cage and made themselves a part of him.

"It's not too late to choose a different life, Caleb."

Chapter Thirteen

Somewhere around the middle of their third Christmas movie, Caleb gently woke Molly where she'd fallen asleep on the couch, a half-eaten cookie in the shape of two gingerbread men 69-ing loosely gripped in her hand, and urged her upstairs to bed. While he brushed his teeth in the bathroom down the hall, she shed her clothing, folding it neatly on top of the dresser in the corner so she could wear it again the next day on their drive home. Molly slipped into the Santa dress she'd stashed in her purse—had that really only been the day before? So much had happened since then... The fuzzy white trim tickled her thighs and chest, but the soft velvet made a perfect nightgown.

She'd just slid beneath the covers when Caleb returned to the room. "Do you—" His gaze snagged on her cleavage, his lips pressing into a flat line. He cleared his throat and looked away, the muscle in his jaw twitching. "Do you want me to turn on the fireplace before you go to sleep?"

"I think I'm okay without it tonight." He nodded and turned towards the door. "Where are you going?"

He gestured down the hall, uncertainty clouding his face. "To the other room."

"Is that what you want?" He hesitated, and she could see him warring with himself behind his hazel eyes. "I didn't put on this very skimpy Christmas dress just to go to bed alone, did I?"

His eyes darkened, sliding over the exposed tops of her breasts again. His Adam's apple bobbed in his throat as he swallowed, his tongue darting out to wet his lips. "It's a good dress. Very...festive."

She flipped back the corner of the covers closest to him. "You could stay here. If this is our last night..." The thought twisted in her stomach, cutting off her breath.

Tomorrow they'd go back to Aster Bay, back to the reality where she couldn't touch him or kiss him, where she'd have to pretend she didn't know the heat of his hands on her skin or the weight of him on her tongue. Tomorrow she'd begin the long, painful process of excising him from her heart. But tonight she could lie in his arms and pretend there was a world in which she wouldn't have to give him up.

He studied her face, and she got the sensation he was seeing every part of her, every forbidden thought and hopeless desire. A grim look of determination settled over his features as he unbuttoned his shirt and stepped out of his pants, leaving him in only his black jersey boxer briefs. He really was far too handsome to be a priest. The muscles of his back and arms rippled as he set his clothes beside her own on the dresser, his glasses neatly on top, and joined her in the bed.

Wrapping an arm around her waist and pulling her back against his front, he settled his lips against the crown of her head. But she wanted to see him, to be closer. She turned in his arms until they were chest to chest, pulling him close and tangling their legs together beneath the cool sheets. His breath was warm on her face, his forehead pressed to hers.

"Do we really have to go back?" she groaned.

"Gavin and the guys might send out a search party if we don't."

She sighed. "Why are our friends so meddlesome?"

"Because they care." He kissed her forehead, feather light. The tenderness of the gesture twisted her heart in her chest. "Because they don't understand why we might wish we could stay."

She tilted her face up to meet his eyes. "Do you? Wish we could stay?"

He smoothed his hand over the back of her head, fingers trailing through her hair like water. "I would stay here forever with you."

It was too much, too heavy, the weight of all the things she needed to say, all the things she wanted and could never have. And when he looked at her like that, like he saw galaxies in her eyes, like he would lasso the moon if she just asked him to—she needed to change the subject or she'd spend their last night together sobbing.

"Even with nothing but frozen pizza and bacon to eat?" she asked.

The corner of his mouth twitched. "Even then."

"Even with just a scraggly Christmas tree and no presents on Christmas morning?"

He pressed his lips against the shell of her ear, his tongue flicking against the lobe. Heat gathered between her thighs. "You are present enough."

"Yeah?" She shifted closer and he slid his hand over her hip, fingers brushing against the curve of her ass.

"Yeah. Especially in this dress."

A breathy laugh bubbled past her lips. "Caleb West, do you have a thing for Santa?"

"I have a thing for you."

His lips were soft and slow as they moved against hers, as though they could do this for the rest of their lives. As though every second that passed wasn't a second closer to the end. He licked into her mouth, gentle and searching, stealing her breath until she was drunk on him.

"What do you want for Christmas, angel?" he whispered into the darkness of the room, lips moving against her throat.

She exhaled a humorless laugh. "More of this. More time."

He slid down her body, lips grazing her collar bone, the tops of her breasts. "We have time," he assured her as he moved lower. His mouth was hot against the velvet covering her belly, the fabric bunching around her hips. "We have so much time."

They both knew it was a lie, but the lie was so sweet and his mouth moving in its slow trek across her body was so distracting...

He nipped at the sensitive skin on the inside of her thigh. "Relax, angel. Let me take care of you."

Time liquefied around her, becoming something soft and slippery. Changeable. Slow. The moon reflected off the snow outside and cast the room in a bluish ethereal glow through the window, like they were under water, floating beneath the waves, suspended weightless where nothing could reach them. Nothing but his clever fingers, the glide of his tongue, the rasp of his stubble between her legs, and then that wave crashed over her, stealing her breath and flooding her senses as she dug her hand into his hair and held his mouth against her.

She lay limp and panting on the sheets as he crawled back up her body, a smug, satisfied sort of quirk to his lips glistening in the moonlight. Nestling her head beneath his chin, he gathered her into his arms and fitted her against him like she had always belonged there. "Caleb?" she murmured, sleep already pulling her under.

"Yeah, Molly?" His voice was hoarse, strained.

She yawned and snuggled closer, her lips brushing against his chest as she spoke, hardly getting the words out before she succumbed to sleep. "I'd stay here forever with you too."

Chapter Fourteen

December 24th
Just after midnight

Caleb held Molly as she slept, her soft exhalations warm against his chest and throat. Sometimes, deep in a dream, her nose would scrunch up and she'd make a little whimpering sound that damn near broke his heart. He pressed his lips to her temple, stroked her hair, whispered that he was there, she wasn't alone, she was safe. He'd keep her safe.

It's not too late to choose a different life.

The first time he'd broached the idea of leaving the priesthood with his confessor was about a year earlier.

It had taken days to work up the courage, to carefully script the things he'd say—he was having doubts about the Church, he was disconnected from God, he'd starting having these thoughts about Molly he couldn't quite shake. Father Raymond had an answer for every one of Caleb's reasons—doubt was normal, his relationship with God was evolving, temptation was a test of faith. Father Raymond had encouraged him to pray on it some more, not to make any rash decisions, and to return when he was ready.

He'd jettisoned the idea to the back of his mind and hadn't brought it up again until last May, the morning after that night in the hall when he'd almost kissed her. This time, he'd gone straight to the Bishop, aware that if Father Raymond told him to reconsider, he would. But the Bishop hadn't been any more eager to see him laicized. The Catholic Church, it turned out, wasn't in the habit of encouraging priests to resign.

Then, a few days ago, after months of conversations, he'd sent off a desperate request to the Diocese for the formal paperwork. Molly had worn a dress with black tights to school. He'd spent the entire morning Mass wondering how easily those tights would rip, how hard he could fuck her on the altar before someone heard them. And yet, when the Bishop had sent his reply and asked him to consider reassignment, it had seemed like a viable option. Maybe leaving Aster Bay—leaving her—would be enough.

He knew better now.

Watching Molly sleep, cherishing the weight of her in his arms and begging time to slow down, he knew simple reassignment would never be enough. Because he didn't want to go back to a life where he couldn't touch her or kiss her whenever he wanted to. A life where they had no future.

I'd stay here forever with you too.

What if Gavin was right? What if God had been sending him signs all along and he'd been too blind to notice? What if this wasn't merely an unexpected snowstorm, but was God's way of forcing Caleb to confront his true feelings head on?

He loved her.

Now, in this moment, certainly, but perhaps for months before.

He was in love with her.

How had it taken him so long to see? Maybe because he'd never been in love before, he'd expected it to arrive with a bang, some life altering thunderclap that could be unmistakably identified. He hadn't expected the slow build, the way his thoughts always turned to her, how he found her in any room no matter how crowded, the strange sense of calm that stole over him each time they were close. He hadn't known loving her could feel like peace and hope and a joy so profound he was almost afraid to feel it fully. And now that he did know, how could he ever go back?

You can't.

Molly sighed happily in her sleep and rolled over, her back to him. He traced her silhouette in the darkness, his palm sliding from rib cage to waist to hip. There was no decision to be made. He'd made it the second he let himself touch her, and he'd make it again a thousand times over.

And now that he'd made it, he didn't want to waste another moment.

Caleb brushed his lips over her shoulder and climbed out of the bed, careful not to wake her. On his way out of the room, he grabbed his glasses and clicked on the small lamp on the bedside table so she wouldn't be alone in the dark. The door closed behind him with a soft snick.

On the opposite side of the hall, he pushed into the small study he'd found earlier in the day. One wall was lined with half-filled bookshelves, a single strand of Christmas garland hanging from a shelf halfway up. The large, floor-to-ceiling window overlooked the motel, beyond which he could see the roads already cleared of snow despite the few flakes continuing to fall. He sank into the burgundy leather wingback chair at the sleek, modern desk and reached for one of the yellow legal pads stacked in the corner. Filing the forms for laicization with the Diocese wouldn't be enough; he'd need to declare his intention to leave the priesthood publicly, in front of enough people the Bishop wouldn't try to change his mind. In front of enough people there would be no taking it back.

Caleb's Christmas Eve homily had been written weeks ago, a cliché message on the blessing of new beginnings and the hope the season offered. Now he knew what was missing: the announcement of his own new beginning. An expression of his gratitude for his parishioners' faith in him, for their grace now as he left them. With each word scribbled on the pad, page after page, he felt lighter, his mind clearer. He promised to continue to pray for his parishioners—asked that they pray for him as well—and, with his pen hovering over the paper, the last words of the homily that would end his career flowing out onto the paper, he felt it.

He closed his eyes, the sensation of warmth and light washing over him, a peace so deep he knew it could only have come from God. He sent up a silent prayer of gratitude—for sending him Molly, for showing him another life, and for releasing him. When the warmth receded, it didn't feel like a loss, but a benediction.

Molly stood in the doorway to the office when he opened his eyes, her hair piled on top of her head in a messy bun and the fur trim on the tiny Santa dress barely brushing the tops of her thighs. "Are you alright?" she asked, her brow drawn low in confusion.

"Better than I've been in years." He set his glasses aside and reached out a hand to her, unable to hold back his smile when she took it. He pulled her close, bringing her to stand between his thighs, holding her at the waist and resting his face against her belly. She smelled like sex and gingerbread.

She raked her hands through his hair. "What are you working on?"

"My homily for Christmas Eve Mass." He lifted his eyes to hers, arms wrapping around her lower back. "It's going to be my last one."

Confusion clouded her face. "Your last what?"

"My last homily. My last Mass."

She blinked, confusion giving way to uncertainty. "Caleb, are you— What are you saying?"

"I'm leaving the priesthood." He exhaled a chuckle. "That feels good to say out loud."

"Are you sure?"

He tugged her into his lap, smoothing the wrinkle between her eyebrows with his thumb. "Yes, I'm sure."

She closed her eyes and took a shaky breath, gripping his hand so tightly her knuckles had turned white. "I don't know how to say this without it sounding incredibly self-centered and presumptuous, so I'm just going to say it."

He grinned. "Alright."

"Is this because of me? Because of what we've done?"

"It's not *not* about you." His grin faltered, but he focused on the amber of her eyes, more golden at the center and darker towards the edge. "I thought you didn't like the Church."

"I don't."

"And you didn't like me working for the Church."

"I know, but I don't want to be the reason you leave."

His stomach dropped and he studied their intertwined hands, her smooth skin and neatly trimmed nails painted with some kind of pale shimmery polish. "Oh."

"It's too much pressure, Caleb. I— it's barely been two days. You can't change your entire life because of two days."

"It hasn't been two days." He set his jaw and met her gaze, willing her to recognize the truth in his words. "It's been eighteen months since I met you, Molly. Eighteen months of feeling like I'll break apart if I don't see you, if I don't talk to you, touch you. Do you have any idea what it's like to spend eighteen months at war with yourself?"

She opened her mouth like she might speak, but then closed it again, glancing away. He needed her to hear him, to understand. He gripped her chin with his thumb and forefinger and tilted her face back up to his.

"I have spent eighteen months begging God to take away these feelings for you, this ache in my chest that never stops. To say nothing for the *years* I've spent praying for Him to help me understand His Church, to help me find my place in it so I could reach the people who needed me. And all it took was two days with you for me to see the answer to both my prayers is the same." He softened his grip, sliding his hand along her jaw to the nape of her neck, the soft hair falling free from her bun tickling the back of his hand. "I cannot change His Church from within it, and so to help the people I've set out to help, I can no longer be a priest." He pressed his forehead to hers. "I cannot stop loving you, and so I can no longer be a priest."

Her breathing hitched, a shuddering exhale moving through her. "You love me?"

"I do. I'm too old for you, I know, and my life is a mess—" Her watery chuckle loosened the tension in his muscles, the last vestiges of his self-preservation falling away. He pulled her into his lap, pressing his hands to her back, the rise and fall of her breathing beneath his palm. "But I love you, Molly Proulx."

Her kiss took him by surprise, the urgency with which she pressed her mouth against his, the demand of her fingers curling in his hair, nails scratching at his scalp. She kissed him as though she needed it to survive, as though she'd draw breath from his lungs, and he'd gladly give it to her. He traced the opening of her mouth with his tongue and she melted against him, the fur at the top of her dress tickling his chest as she moved in his lap.

They broke apart, panting, her lips swollen and eyes bright. "Say it again."

"I lo—"

"I love you too." The glow of her smile was a gift he didn't deserve but would gladly accept. "And you really don't want to be a priest anymore? You're sure you want to leave?"

He slid his hands down her back, adjusting her in his lap so she was straddling his thighs and gripping her ass through the thin velvet dress. "I'm sure, angel."

"But what about—"

He cut off her question with a crushing kiss, quick but firm. "I don't have all the answers yet, Mol, but I know what I want." He settled her against him, urging her forward so she could feel the thick ridge of his erection trapped in his boxer briefs beneath her. He knew the moment she felt it because her pupils widened and she bit her lip, that simple gesture making him painfully harder. "I want to help people, the way I always intended to. And I want a life where I can love you with all my heart, all my soul, and all my body."

She rocked against him, teasing him with the slow roll of her hips. "It'll cause a scandal in a town as small as Aster Bay, a priest falling from grace."

"Not falling from grace," he said, hands sliding under her skirt to caress the soft skin hiding there. "Just falling in love."

Would he ever get used to seeing her smile like this, warm and secretive, like she knew exactly what she was doing to him and found it delightful? "We'll figure the rest of it out together. If you'll have me."

"As if you could get rid of me now," she said, bending to kiss him.

Then she was gone from his lap, standing over him as she slowly lifted the hem of her ridiculous Santa costume and pulled it over her head. The scrap of fabric landed on the floor at her feet. He couldn't keep himself from reaching for her, couldn't believe the blessing of being able to see her like this, naked and needy and wanting *him.* He lifted her breast to his lips, sucking the furled tip into his mouth, desperate to taste her everywhere.

But Molly had plans of her own, it seemed. She tugged at the waist of his boxer briefs and he lifted his hips to allow her pull them down his legs. He thickened under her hungry gaze, and he circled the base of his shaft with one hand, stroking himself slowly, gripping tightly. "Sit on the desk," he said, his voice rough with desire.

She complied, sliding her bottom onto the edge of the desk and letting her knees drop to the side. She was a vision, glistening and pink, her thighs red from his stubble when he'd licked her to orgasm earlier in the night. He loved seeing the evidence that he'd been between her legs once already that night, the proof she wanted him there again.

He placed her feet on his knees, then spread his legs wide, moving hers apart at the same time, as he settled back in the chair. The new angle put more of her on display, the sight of her waiting and open for him sending a thrum of power through his veins. He returned his hand to his cock, stroking slowly, his other hand holding her foot in place on his knee.

"You are such a gift," he whispered.

Holding his gaze, her hand drifted over her thigh. His eyes zeroed in on the movement as she dragged a finger through her seam, swirling around her clit, then moved lower, gathering wetness. Again and again, each stroke slower, more purposeful than the last.

"Let me see you," he said, a broken plea.

She used the spread V of her index and middle finger to open herself further for him, putting every part of herself on display, the glistening place where he would slide in, stretching her, filling her, the swollen bud begging for his attention.

He released a shuddering breath, leaning closer and squeezing his cock against the urgent need to fuck her. "Oh, angel, you are so beautiful." With his free hand, he reached forward and pressed two fingers inside her, settling his thumb against her clit as she continued to hold herself open for him. "I want to feel you come. Can I make you come, Molly?"

She nodded, chest rising and falling faster as he explored her with his fingers. "Yes, Father."

His cock kicked in his hand, heat racing down his spine, and her pussy clenched around his fingers when she used his title. "Dirty girl," he chided, curling his fingers within her.

She laughed breathlessly, her hips rocking up to meet his touch. "I want to come on your cock," she whispered.

He groaned, dropping his forehead to her knee and pressing his lips there. "I don't have a condom, Molly."

"I have an IUD and I was tested recently." He lifted questioning eyes to hers. "If it's okay with you... Caleb, It's all I've thought about for months. Please—"

He surged forward, pulling her face down to his and crashing his mouth against hers as he continued to finger her. That this woman had been thinking about him in this way, that she wanted him so much, trusted him enough— It was almost more than he could take. She came on his hand, her hips moving restlessly in time with his fingers and a little cry escaping around their kiss. He had to be inside her, to feel the grip of her inner muscles on his cock, to feel her everywhere.

He pushed her feet off his knees and tugged her into his lap, settling her so she straddled his thighs, his hands planted on her ass. She rested her arms on his shoulders and lifted up, allowing him to notch himself at her entrance. The tip of his cock pressed inside her, the hot clutch of her body overwhelming, and he threw his head back, clenching his jaw to keep himself from coming before he was even all the way inside. Slowly she lifted up and lowered herself back down, over and over, taking him a fraction of an inch at a time. She was so tight, so warm, so soft—

She lowered herself a tiny bit more, a shiver passing down her spine. "You're too big," she whispered.

"You can take it." He moved one hand around her hip and used his thumb to stroke her clit. As he did, she relaxed around him, her body making room for him. "That's it, love. You can do it. It'll fit." By degrees, he slid deeper until he was seated to the hilt inside the heaven of her body. "Our bodies were made for this. See how well you take me?"

She glanced between them at the thick intrusion of his cock buried inside her, but he knew from that angle only he could truly see how beautifully she'd stretched for him, the magnificent way her body had made space to welcome him inside.

"Caleb," she whimpered, rocking against him, "I need..."

"I know, love." He moved his hand back to her ass, stifling a grin when she made a little sound of protest as his finger left her clit. "You are so needy, angel. Take what you need." With his grip on her ass, he lifted her slightly in his lap, then lowered her back down, urging her to ride him.

She didn't need much encouragement. As she bounced on his cock, her breasts shook, tempting him to capture them with his mouth. She moved faster, rising up higher and slamming down harder, and he dug his hands into her ass, pulling her cheeks apart as he helped her come down harder each time. He slid lower in the chair, and a look of wonder crossed her face, her eyes falling shut and her mouth pulling into that perfect little O as the new angle drove his cock into a new place deep inside her.

"Are you going to come for me, Molly?" He gritted his teeth as his own orgasm barreled down his spine, determined not to come before she did. "Let me feel it, love."

"Come with me. I want you to come inside me."

He pulled her down as his hips drove up into her, hard and deep, until sparks flew over his skin. He was so close, and the idea of coming inside her, of pumping her full of his cum and watching it drip out of her swollen pussy before he pushed it back inside, of doing it again and again for the rest of their lives—

His vision went white around the edges as her pussy clamped down on his length and pulled his orgasm from him. He fucked her as she shook in his arms, her climax a grasping, greedy thing, swallowing every burst of his release. His lungs burned with the need to catch his breath as each new wave of bliss rioted through him. At last, her movements slowed, the aftershocks of her orgasm sending pulses of unexpected pleasure through his spent cock, their bodies slick with sweat and sticky where they were joined.

He kissed her, holding her in place on his lap, still buried deep inside her, and knowing *this* was what Molly meant when she talked about sex that could change you. Because there was no denying he was changed, every part of him broken apart and put back together by the act of loving her. He'd spend the rest of his life watching pleasure bloom across her skin and knowing he was the cause, knowing she had altered every part of him, and thanking God for it.

Chapter Fifteen

For the second morning in a row, Molly woke to find Caleb gone. Sometime in the early hours of the morning, tired and sore and hazy from their orgasms, they'd climbed back into bed, falling asleep curled together as though they'd done it a thousand times before.

It had been a perfect night.

But when she rolled over in the morning and was greeted by the cold sheets on his side of the bed, something seemed off. A tiny ripple of nerves across the back of her neck, the most miniscule curl of doubt in her stomach.

That whisper at the back of her mind that something had shifted while she was sleeping followed her as she dressed in days old clothing, dogged her heels as she trotted down the stairs, seemed to echo through the empty cabin when her foot landed on the creaky bottom step.

"Caleb?" she called.

He wasn't in the living room or the kitchen, but a freshly brewed pot of coffee sat in the coffee maker, a clean mug set beside it waiting for her, his dirty one rinsed and resting in the drainer tray by the sink. She told herself she was being silly as she poured cream into her coffee and stirred in the sugar. He'd probably just gone to dig out the car, or to settle their bill at the motel. Taking her coffee to sit on the couch in the living room, she let the heavy ceramic warm her hands as she replayed the day before, the way he'd kissed her against the wall by the tree, how he'd laid her out and licked her to orgasm in front of the fire, the little touches and kisses and flirtations. The hunger in his eyes when she'd climbed on the desk the night before, the confusing mix of tenderness and possessiveness with which he'd fucked her.

The front door flew open and Caleb came in, stamping his feet to clear them of the snow clinging to his shoes. He blew on his hands to warm them and her foolish heart kickstarted. She knew the moment he caught sight of her, his eyes twinkling behind his glasses and a slow grin spreading over his face. He scrubbed a hand through his hair, dislodging snowflakes. "Good morning."

Why his simple greeting made her blush, she'd never know. The man had been inside of her the night before, for Christ's sake.

"Good morning," she said, finally taking a sip of her coffee to try to hide the dirty thoughts flooding her brain.

"What's that look for?" he asked as he shrugged out of his jacket.

His clerical collar gleamed bright white against the black of his shirt. She'd almost forgotten how stark the contrast was in the hours since he'd removed it. The sight of that stupid piece of plastic made the curl of doubt in her stomach stretch and spread, slinging itself lazily over her organs and twining itself with her ribs as it crawled up towards her throat.

Of course he's wearing his collar. We're headed back to Aster Bay, and he is a priest.

For now.

The reminder of his plan to quit only partially quelled the anxiety spiraling out of control within her.

But Caleb didn't seem to notice. Ever practical, he called from the kitchen as he got himself a glass of water, "The car's plowed out and cleaned off, and we're paid up with the front desk. We should get on the road soon. If we leave now, we'll be back in Aster Bay with a few hours to spare before the Christmas Eve Mass. I need to go over some things with Father Murphy before parishioners start arriving, and you know how Mrs. Greene and the Grandma Gang love to show up twenty minutes early to everything." He reappeared at the entry to the living room. She must have been making a face because confusion clouded his expression, and he leaned against the doorway. "Unless you wanted to shower before we go?"

She shook away the anxious thoughts and got to her feet, downing the last of her coffee as she headed for the kitchen. "No, you're right. I'm ready."

As she passed him, he caught her around the waist, slowing her progress. He scanned her face as he drew light circles on her lower back with his fingertips. "Hey, are you alright?"

"Yeah, of course. Just tired. Someone kept me up all night," she teased before dropping a quick peck on his cheek and moving out of his hold to rinse her coffee cup.

He didn't ask again as they gathered their few belongings and navigated the narrow cleared through the snow from The Stable's door to the parking lot. The roads were empty and quiet as Caleb steered his little car towards the highway, the backseat loaded with trash bags full of costumes. It would be the perfect time to tell him about her job offer. If he was really going to leave the Church, she could turn it down. She'd leave St. Anthony's High, but she could find another teaching position somewhere closer to Aster Bay. They could start over together.

You cannot plan your life around his.

"Do you think Bruce will be happy with the costumes?" Caleb asked.

"I expect he'll burn the Santa suits and elf hats in some sort of ritual sacrifice."

He laughed, the sound sweeping away some of the strange tension clinging to her. She wasn't sure why she was so out of sorts this morning. After the night they'd had, she should have been ecstatic, dreaming of the future that lay before them, the one she had never dared to hope for. But she couldn't quite shake this sense of foreboding, like something wasn't quite right and she just couldn't see it yet.

"Will you come to Mass tonight?" he asked.

The nerves in his tone pulled her up short. She angled her body towards him as she answered carefully. "I haven't been to a Mass outside of school hours in a long time." He nodded, breathing deeply, and kept his eyes on the road, almost as if he was afraid to look at her. "But if you want me there—"

"I do." He glanced at her, something like relief flashing in the gold flecks of his eyes. "I mean, I'd like you to hear the homily I wrote. If you want to."

"Then I'll be there."

He smiled, reaching over to take her hand. Their clasped hands rested on her knee, fingers intertwined. He wanted her to hear him preach his last homily, and so she would. He wanted to hold her hand, and so he did. *Simple. This can be simple. Stop overthinking it.*

"Will you go to Lemon and Thyme after Mass?" she asked. Their friends Jamie and Tessa hosted a big family dinner at their restaurant every Christmas Eve. It was her favorite part of the holiday. This year, since Caleb had to preach, they'd decided to move the dinner to after Mass.

"I think Gavin might kill me if I don't." For a moment, he looked like he had more to say, but stopped himself.

The entire drive was like that—conversation in fits and starts. She wanted to go back to bed and start the day over, to slough off whatever this unease was that had taken up residence between them, to go back to cuddling and kissing and talking about the future. But his mind was on the upcoming service and she couldn't help but worry about what that meant. What if he got back to St. Anthony's and realized he wasn't ready to leave the priesthood after all? What if he slipped back into the role of Father West and left behind the man he'd been for the last two days?

Was two days really enough to change a life?

"Are you nervous for tonight?" she asked.

"A little. I don't think I've been nervous about giving a homily in a decade at least. But this one is different." He squeezed her hand and shot her a grin, the curve of his lip beating back the tendrils of doubt.

"You love what you do," she said softly, unsure whether it was a question or a statement.

"I—" He hesitated, the furrow between his brows making a brief appearance. "I have loved many things about what I do."

"Like preaching?"

"Like helping people feel close to God. Like being there for the biggest moments of their lives—the weddings and baptisms and deaths. It's a privilege to walk with them in those moments." The furrow in her brown deepened. "That reminds me. I need to make sure Father Murphy knows to bring his blue rosary beads with him when he visits the assisted living facility. Mrs. Johnson thinks red rosary beads are a bad omen. Oh! And I'll have to warn him not to eat the cookies in Mrs. Faria's room. I almost chipped a tooth the last time she offered me one." He pointed at one his front teeth.

"Will you miss it?"

He blew out a breath, his lips pursing out with his exhalation. She knew what those lips tasted like now, the warm glide of them on the inside of her thighs...

"I'm sure there are things I will miss, but I'm also sure I can find a hundred new ways to be a safe place for people without sacrificing such large parts of myself to do it."

It was a perfect answer. Textbook perfect. Still...

When, at last, Caleb pulled into the little parking lot behind St. Anthony's Church four hours later, hers was the only other car in the lot. They wrestled the garbage bags of costumes out of the car and dragged them down the stone steps to the small office area in the basement of the church. The bags safely stowed in the corner of the office for when school reopened, Molly clapped her hands together and glanced around the overstuffed office. "Well, I guess I'll see you tonight."

"Hey." Caleb leaned against his desk, piles of papers and sticky notes covering every surface, and rested his hands on her hips, drawing her closer. "What's going on? You've been off all morning."

She blew out a frustrated breath and shook her head. "I'm sorry. I'm just in my head."

He tilted his face down until they were eye level, looking up at her through his thick eyelashes. "You can talk to me. You know that, right?"

She lifted a finger and tentatively tugged on his collar, not enough to dislodge it, but enough to remind herself it could come off. His eyes narrowed, and she could practically see the gears turning in his brain.

"You're giving up so much. And I'm not giving up anything."

"I suspect you'll need to find a new job once Bruce finds out you're shacked up with a defrocked priest."

She shoved against his chest lightly, a reluctant smile on her lips. "I'm giving up a job. You're giving up who you are."

"No, not who I am." He pulled her closer, moving her between his legs. "I have been more myself in the last two days with you than I have been in years. I'm not giving up who I am. I'm reclaiming it." She nodded, letting his reassurance quiet the lingering wisps of worry in her mind. "Give me a few hours. Come to Mass tonight. Trust me."

She straightened his lapel, tucking his collar back into place, and smiled wryly. "I wish I could kiss you right now," she whispered.

He mimicked her with a too-loud whisper of his own. "Why can't you?"

Her eyes went wide. "We're in your church."

He glanced around the room. "We're the only ones here." And there was that grin again, the one that sent butterflies fluttering in her stomach and heaviness gathering between her legs. He dragged his fingers along the waistband of her jeans, hooking them in her belt loops, and tugged. "Come here, angel."

His kiss was slow and decadent. She focused on the scratch of his two-day-old stubble, the sharp sting of his teeth tugging on her bottom lip before he soothed the bite with the languid glide of his tongue. "Stop thinking so hard, Molly," he rasped against her lips.

She chuckled, delighted by how well he knew her even as her own mind was at war with itself. He trailed his lips down the column of her throat, his hands slipping into the back pockets of her jeans and pulling her forward until they were hip to hip. Holding him to her with fingers tangled in his hair, she sighed. "Last night...we didn't discuss how this is all going to work."

"We got a little distracted." She could feel his smile against her skin.

"I guess I'm a details kind of girl. Without knowing how, it's hard for me to believe I didn't imagine it."

He paused in his exploration of her throat, a smile lighting up his face despite the seriousness in his eyes. "You didn't imagine it." He took her hand and pressed it against his chest, holding it there so she could feel the pounding of his heart beneath his shirt. "Here's how this is going to work. Tonight, I'm going to preach my last homily at Christmas Eve Mass. Then you and I are going to family dinner to celebrate with our friends. And tomorrow, we'll figure out what comes next. And the day after that, and the day after that, for the rest of our lives." Her surprise must have shown on her face because he released a low, throaty chuckle and dropped a quick kiss on her lips. "Too soon?"

The creak of the door to the stairwell down the hall resounded through the room and they leapt apart, Molly spinning in a circle as she looked for a reason to be alone with

Caleb in his office. For his part, Caleb seemed much less fazed by almost getting caught wrapped in each other's arms. He bit back a smile as he adjusted the bulge in his pants and took a seat at his desk, the oversized wooden hand-me-down conveniently concealing his erection.

"Father West?" The voice of Father Murphy, St. Anthony's associate pastor, rang out only moments before the door to the office burst open. The older man looked out of breath, his silver combover sticking up in odd places as though he'd tried to run his hands through the sparse hair left on his head. "What is this email?" he demanded.

"Good afternoon, Father Murphy. You remember Ms. Proulx from the High School," Caleb said, gesturing to Molly.

Father Murphy nodded in her direction, then snapped his attention back to Caleb. "We need to talk."

"I can go," Molly said, moving towards the door.

"You don't need to leave," Caleb said. "This will only take a minute." Father Murphy's nostrils flared, clearly annoyed.

"I think there's one more bag of angel wings in the car. I'll just go get it and then I'll come back." With an uneasy glance at Father Murphy, she added, "Take your time," before scurrying from the room, leaving the two priests to hash out whatever the hell that was.

She took her time climbing the steps to the parking lot, then leaned against Caleb's car and took out her phone to buy some time. She'd missed a string of messages in the group chat while she'd been busy kissing Caleb in the basement of his church.

Jo: Molly, where are you? I thought you were going to be home in time to go shopping. I need to get a present for Julie.

Tessa: My daughter doesn't need anything from anyone. Her room is already overflowing.

Kyla: As if that's going to stop Jo.

Sabrina: Or any of us, really. Sebastian and I already bought her a giant stuffed hedgehog.

Hannah: Why a hedgehog?

Sabrina: It's three feet wide and the softest thing ever. Sebastian named it Hedgie, but don't tell him I told you that.

Jo: See! I cannot be outdone in the best auntie contest.

Tessa: It's not a contest.

Jo: It's always a contest.

Kyla: I'll go shopping with you. Gavin and Brodie are having some father-son bonding time, so I'm sure they wouldn't mind if I left the house for a bit.

Hannah: I want to go too. Ethan already picked out a carload of toys for Julie, but I want to get her something special just from me.

Tessa: I'm never going to have a clean house again, am I?

Jo: Please. You never had a clean house to begin with.

Molly grinned. Maybe all she needed was to be back home with their chaotic little friend family to remember even the most fraught beginnings could have a happy ending. If Tessa and her father's best friend could do it, and Kyla and her ex-boyfriend's father could do it, and Sabrina and her sister's ex-fiancé could do it, and Hannah and Ethan could survive the press scrutiny— if all of her friends could figure it out, then dammit, so could she and Caleb.

Right?

Molly: We're back. Dropping some things off at St. Anthony's. I'll be home soon.

Jo: Woo! Girls' trip to the toy store!

Sabrina: I think we should clarify which kind of toy store you're planning on us going to.

Jo: Both kinds. One for the adorable little munchkin we all love so much, and one for us to spoil ourselves.

Tessa: I can't go. I told Jamie I'd help him prep for tonight's family dinner. You guys have fun without me.

Tessa: And, Jo, make sure you don't mix up the toy store bags when you wrap Julie's gift.

Jo: No worries. That's a mistake you only make once.

Kyla: Can we have one scandal-free holiday, please?

Jo: Define scandal free?

Hannah: No inappropriate photos ending up online.

Kyla: No Grandma Gang cornering my husband to get details about one of our relationships.

Jo: They wouldn't corner Gavin if he didn't fold every time Mrs. Greene gave him the stink eye.

Kyla: Just one holiday where we're all together and happy and no drama.

Tessa: And no sex toys at the dinner table.

Jo: That was one time!

Molly tucked her phone back in her purse. A scandal-free holiday meant no waltzing into family dinner holding a priest's hand. Which was fine. She could keep this to herself until after Christmas. Probably.

Sure enough, there was one trash bag left in the trunk of Caleb's car, an iridescent angel wing poking out of the opening. She slung the bag over her shoulder and headed back into the church basement, determined to say her goodbyes quickly and get home to keep her promise to the girls. It was time to go back to reality.

"You're being selfish," Father Murphy's raised voice pulled Molly up short outside the door to Caleb's office. She set the bag down on the floor and paused, unsure whether she should knock or go back outside and give the two priests some more time.

"I appreciate your perspective, but—"

"You cannot do this. You will make a mockery of this parish," Father Murphy said, cutting off Caleb's reply. "You aren't thinking clearly. I knew the moment I got your email this morning something was off, and then I find you with that woman—"

"She has a name."

Molly held her breath, shame crawling up her throat and heating her cheeks.

"This is not the time. Your parishioners deserve better from you. Don't do something rash you'll regret when you've had time to think it through."

A long silence. Then, "You're right."

Molly dropped the bag at her feet, angel wings spilling out onto the beige carpet. She'd been here before, had been delivered a similar warning she'd been too naive to listen to—and she knew how it ended. The smart thing to do would be to leave, to get in her car and drive far away, to accept the job offer waiting in her inbox, to start looking for apartments in Boston and never look back.

But her feet wouldn't move. No matter how badly she wanted to disappear and pretend she hadn't heard a thing, she wanted Caleb more.

Father Murphy's booming voice, now calmer, came through the door. "Of course, I'm right. You'll see. Leave the impulsive decisions to the youth."

"Thank you for your counsel, Father Murphy."

The door to the office swung open and Father Murphy startled at the sight of her. He scanned the mess of angel wings at her feet. "Ms. Proulx, let me help you," he said, bending to retrieve a particularly glittery set of wings.

"That's alright. I've got it." She flashed a weak smile.

He seemed skeptical but he nodded and made his way down the hall, careful not to step on any of the wings on his way by.

Father Murphy disappeared through the door to the parking lot, but Molly waited until she'd counted to ten in her head before entering Caleb's office, wings littering the hallway. Caleb was still seated behind his desk, but his lips were turned down in a pensive frown, the crease between his eyebrows more prominent.

His eyes softened when he saw her. "There you are. I was beginning to wonder if you got lost." He sounded tired. Had he sounded so tired before Father Murphy's visit?

"I couldn't help but overhear..." She gestured towards the door half-heartedly.

Caleb sighed, running his thumb and index finger over his eyes behind his glasses. "Father Murphy means well."

"Maybe he has a point. Maybe we are making a rash decision."

"What?" All traces of exhaustion disappeared from his face, his frame stiff and alert, as though he was preparing to leap out of his chair. "Molly, that's not—"

"I'm not saying we're wrong," she rushed to add, "but I think we need to take a beat."

"A beat," he repeated, incredulous.

"Some space."

He pushed his chair back and rounded on her in one swift movement, taking her hand in both of his. "I don't want space."

She swallowed around the lump in her throat. "I think we should do it anyway."

His mouth fell open, a puff of air leaving his lungs. "Is that what you want?"

Of course it wasn't! Her throat constricted, tears stinging her nose and the backs of her eyes. She wanted him, every moment of him, but not if he wasn't sure. Not if one conversation with Father Murphy was enough to have him wavering. She wanted all of him, every moment, but they'd been so caught up in the last two days, in the dream come to life, maybe they weren't thinking clearly. And she loved him enough to give him the chance to change his mind.

"I know what it's like to have someone regret changing their life for me."

"Molly—"

"I don't think I could take it if you ever looked at me that way. And I don't want to ever look at you that way either."

"What are you talking about?"

"I have a job offer," she blurted as she dashed away a tear. "A really great job offer. In Boston."

"You what?" He sounded like all the air had been knocked out of his lungs and his face went white. "Why didn't you tell me?"

"I haven't decided whether or not I'm going to take it yet. This is all happening so fast. We could both use a minute to be sure this is the right decision. I don't want to repeat the same mistakes I've already made. I don't want to wake up in three years and wonder if we rushed into changing our whole lives. You're too important—this is too important for that."

The muscle in his jaw twitched, the sparkle gone from his eyes. "Why does it feel like you're saying goodbye?"

"Not goodbye. Just some space to be sure."

Her hand slipped from his grasp and he stumbled back a step, looking like he'd just been sucker punched. "If that's what you need."

She dashed away a tear and left, telling herself it was the smart decision, that a break wasn't a *breakup*. Her feet slid on the gossamer angel wings as she fled the church, tears streaming down her face and her heart screaming for her to go back. She fumbled with her keys, turning out of the parking lot on autopilot, but she was crying too hard to drive. She pulled over on the side of the road a few blocks from the church, the steeple with its stained-glass window taking up most of her rearview mirror, and for the first time in years, she prayed.

Chapter Sixteen

"What are you still doing down here?"

Caleb looked up from his computer at the sound of Father Murphy's voice. The office was dim, lit only by the small lamp on his desk and the blue glow from his computer screen. When had the sun gone down? How long had he been sitting in this room fumbling through paperwork and hoping Molly would come back? Why hadn't she told him about her job offer? Would she really move to Boston?

"What time is it?" he asked.

"It's nearly seven o'clock. The Church is full and you're not even wearing your chasuble yet." The older priest tsked.

Caleb glanced at his computer screen, the open email to the Bishop's office staring back at him. Just a few clicks and it would be done. Just a few clicks and this would be the last time he'd put on his vestments.

Was Molly somewhere also changing her life with a few clicks?

"Have you sent it in?" Father Murphy asked.

"I needed to speak with the Superintendent first. Now that's done, I was just about to."

"Then you've taken my advice."

Caleb gave a wan smile at Father Murphy's obvious relief. "I have. Thank you for your counsel. The last thing I want to do is cause additional distress to the parishioners by hijacking their Christmas Eve service for my own needs." His smile faded. "I suppose I had some romantic notions about grand gestures and happily ever afters."

"And your young woman..."

"Molly." Even saying her name made his stomach flip.

"Molly. She wanted a grand gesture?"

He shook his head. "She didn't know what I was planning. But given she didn't want me to quit for her..." *Maybe she doesn't even actually want this life with me...* "It's better this way. Less showy."

Father Murphy studied him, years of hearing confessions and providing counsel to the parishioners at St. Anthony making him too observant. "You wanted the show."

"I love her. I would shout it from every pulpit in the country if I thought it would help her believe it."

Father Murphy hummed in thought. "I fell in love once."

Caleb's attention snapped to the older priest. "You—what?"

"Deirdre O'Brough. The summer after I took my vows, she was visiting family for the summer. She had wild red curls and freckles like you've never seen before." Father Murphy smiled, lost in the memory.

"What happened?"

"Nothing quite as interesting as you and your Molly. It was little more than a flirtation, one kiss behind the giant maple tree out back. And I tortured myself over it. How could I be so newly ordained and already a woman could turn my head?" Father Murphy handed Caleb his alb, watching him with that too-keen attention as the younger priest donned the garment. "I told my confessor, and do you know what he said?"

"What?"

"If you aren't falling in love with someone at least once a decade, you aren't trying hard enough to see God within them." Father Murphy chuckled at Caleb's shocked expression. "I think he may have been exaggerating a little so I would stop beating myself up over poor Deirdre, but in the end, he was right. I didn't love her as a man loves a woman. I loved her because the presence of God within her was so visible. Right there on the surface. And so, at the end of the summer, we said our goodbyes."

Caleb considered Father Murphy's story as he draped the stole around his shoulders, making sure both ends were even and lying flat.

"Before you walk away from the work you've devoted twenty-five years of your life to, Father West, are you sure you love her for more than just the presence of God within her?"

He didn't even need to think about it. "I am. I have tried not to love her," he admitted with a sad tilt of his lips. "I must confess, though, Father, that even if I had been successful, it would still be time for me to leave. She reminded me of all the parts of myself I've been suppressing to fit what the Church has asked me to be, and now I see it, I can't unsee it."

"Then I suppose I can't convince you to reconsider leaving us." Father Murphy handed Caleb the hanger with his chasuble. The white and gold vestment was heavier than Caleb remembered.

Caleb hit the button on his computer that sent his resignation and formal request for laicization to the Bishop's office, immediately feeling lighter. "This will be my last Mass, whether the Bishop is ready to grant me dispensation or not. Though I am sorry for leaving you to manage on your own until the Diocese sends you a new pastor."

Father Murphy smiled. "We will manage, Father West. And my sister will be thrilled to hear me preach on Christmas Day."

Caleb chuckled.

"And your Molly?" Father Murphy asked.

A familiar pang of longing wiped the smile from Caleb's face. *His Molly.* Was she still his? "That may take some more time to sort out."

"Far be it from me to tell you what to do, but if you will indulge me for just one more piece of advice tonight—remember Corinthians. Love is patient. It always protects, always trusts, always hopes, always perseveres," Father Murphy said, clapping Caleb on the back. "And so must you, my friend."

He knew Father Murphy was right, and yet he couldn't help feeling unsettled.

It will be fine. She'll come to Mass, you'll go to dinner with your friends, and you'll talk it all out. She got cold feet, that's all. It will be fine.

But when Caleb took to the altar at St. Anthony's for the last time and looked out over the congregation, Molly wasn't there.

Chapter Seventeen

"We have Chubby Hubby and Phish Food." Jo held up two bowls of ice cream.

From her seat on the couch, Molly snuggled deeper under the chenille blanket. "I can't decide. You pick."

"As if I'd make you choose," Jo scoffed. She handed a bowl to Molly. "You've got two scoops of each."

Molly gratefully accepted the bowl, swirling her spoon to get just the right combination of peanut butter and caramel in one bite. On the TV, *While You Were Sleeping* played, Bill Pullman giving Sandra Bullock his iconic speech about the implications of leaning in during a conversation. Jo flopped down on the couch next to her, digging her freezing cold toes under one edge of the blanket.

She really was the best friend. Jo had taken one look at Molly when she returned home from St. Anthony's and sent a nonsensical message to the group chat calling off their last-minute shopping spree. Instead, she'd thrown the blanket at Molly and placed an order for the largest, cheesiest pizza on the Pizza Stone's menu and two pints of the hard stuff: Ben and Jerry's.

Jo nudged Molly with her toe. "So, are you going to tell me what happened?"

"Nothing happened."

"Bullshit. Molly Marie Proulx—"

"That's not my middle name."

"—Something happened in that cabin."

Heat crept up her throat. "Let's just watch the movie."

Jo grabbed the remote and paused the movie. "Screw the movie. Spoiler alert: Bill Pullman is charming and gets the girl because Bill Pullman is *always* charming and gets the girl. What happened in that cabin, Mol? I need to know if I should suit up and kick some hot priest ass or what."

"Don't kick anyone's ass." Molly took a large bite of ice cream as she mulled over what to say, her tongue stinging from the cold. "Jo, I..."

"I knew it!" Jo screeched, jumping up so she was kneeling on the couch. She lunged at Molly, wrapping her arms around her in the biggest hug. "I knew you two were supposed to be together! Tell me everything. Was the sex amazing? I bet the sex was amazing. Dirty, forbidden sex always is."

"I can't breathe," Molly laughed, shoving her friend back to her own side of the couch.

"Holy shit, Mol, you banged the hot priest."

Molly nodded, tears suddenly springing to her eyes again.

"Hey, what's going on? Why are you crying? I swear to God, if he hurt you—"

"He didn't do anything. He's... It's me, Jo. I'm—I'm a mess. What am I even doing? I'm in love with a *priest?* And now he wants to leave the Church and it's all my fault and—"

"Woah, slow down. You're in love with him?"

"Yeah. Isn't that what we're talking about?" Molly dashed away a tear and poked at her ice cream, but even Chubby Hubby couldn't make her feel better this time. She set the bowl down on the coffee table.

"I thought you two were fucking. I didn't know you were in love." Molly shot her an exasperated look, but Jo pushed ahead. "Wait, he wants to leave the priesthood for you? Isn't that a good thing?"

"It's only been two days. He can't change everything about his life because of two days. That's insane. He's going to regret it, and then he'll blame me."

"What would be insane is to pretend like you two haven't been all about each other for over a year now." It was so much like what Caleb had said it knocked the air from Molly's lungs. "He's not your ex, Molly. Caleb is a grown man who clearly isn't afraid to commit, so what I can't figure out is why you're here eating Ben and Jerry's with me instead of off somewhere being in love with Caleb."

"What about my job offer in Boston?"

Jo scoffed. "Please, as if you were ever really going to leave me, the most perfect roommate ever, and move to Boston."

Molly shook her head, her own argument beginning to crack under her friend's analysis. "It's too fast."

"Why?"

"I don't know! This is important, Jo. I... If you love someone, set them free."

"Bullshit. If you love someone, fight like hell for them."

Maybe Jo was right. Maybe they didn't need space—maybe they needed to hold hands and jump into the abyss.

"I told him we needed to give each other some space, so he could be sure of what he wants."

"It sounds like he *is* sure. Are you?"

"I love him," she sobbed.

Jo pulled her into a hug, her hold surprisingly tight for such a petite woman. "Oh, babe, then why are you crying?"

"I messed it up. I got scared and I pushed him away and—"

"Then tell him that. Spoiler alert, he's pretty good at forgiving people—it was kind of his whole job. Molly, that man wants to flip his world upside down because he loves you. He gets to make that choice. You just have to let him."

By the time her tears finally stopped coming and their ice cream was fully melted, Molly got an idea. It might be a little crazy, but this whole thing was crazy, wasn't it? She was in love with a priest! But the more she let the idea unfurl in her mind, the more perfect it seemed.

She turned to Jo, who was preoccupied fishing chocolate covered pretzels out of her ice cream soup. "I need your help with something—something to show Caleb I'm willing to fight for him. For us."

A smile spread across Jo's lips. "Hell yeah. Let's grand gesture the shit out of that man."

Chapter Eighteen

"**I**s she here?"

All eyes turned to Caleb where he stood trying to catch his breath in the doorway at Lemon and Thyme. His friends were already gathered around the cluster of tables Jamie and Tessa had pushed together to accommodate their large number, the smell of rosemary, sage, and garlic hanging in the air. Caleb scanned everyone gathered around Ethan and Hannah. He'd clearly interrupted something, but he was struggling to care. Molly hadn't shown up at Mass and if she also wasn't at family dinner...

"Is who here?" Tessa asked, glancing around.

"Molly."

Gavin moved towards his brother, holding out a wine glass. "No, she and Jo haven't gotten here yet. Why don't you come in and have a drink?"

"I don't want a drink." He shrugged off his brother's well-intentioned hand on his shoulder as he headed for his sister-in-law, the person in the room who knew Molly best. "Is she coming?"

Kyla's eyes grew wide and darted between the other women, as though the answer to Caleb's question might be written on their foreheads. "I—I think so. She didn't say anything about not coming tonight."

"She and Jo did cancel our shopping trip, though," Sabrina offered.

"Did you try calling her?" Tessa asked.

"She didn't answer," Caleb said. "She said she'd come to Mass, but she didn't. And now she's not here either—"

"What happened?" Gavin asked.

"I don't know! One minute we were great and the next—"

"We?" Ethan's eyebrows shot up his forehead.

Caleb looked between his friends, each of them madly in love with someone who, on paper, they weren't supposed to be with. Each of them happier than he'd ever seen them. His attention caught on Hannah's hand, held out in front of the other women. "Is that—Did you guys get engaged?"

Ethan's chest puffed up, a grin spreading across his face. "We did."

"Congratulations." He wanted to be happier for them, to celebrate with them, but all he could think about was the very real possibility he'd never get the chance to propose to Molly. She was running away and he couldn't figure out how to stop her.

"Wait, we're not talking about them right now. Sorry, guys," Jamie said to Ethan before turning back to Caleb. "Right now, we're talking about you and Molly and why you're bursting into family dinner like someone set your house on fire."

"She—I—"

Where was he even supposed to start?

"He's in love with her," Gavin answered for him.

"Obviously." Baz took a sip of his Scotch, arching an eyebrow at Caleb over the glass as though he dared the priest to argue with his assessment of the situation.

"But that's a good thing!" Kyla squealed. Then, taking in Caleb's tortured expression, "Right? I mean, she's in love with you too."

"You all have just *known* this?" Caleb sputtered.

"Pretty much," Sabrina said as she took a seat on Baz's lap. Baz smiled at her in a way he reserved solely for his wife. Caleb's chest burned with an uncomfortable mix of envy and longing.

Just then, all of the women's phones dinged at once, a cacophony of electronic notifications sounding. "So much for a scandal-free holiday. We have to go," Kyla said as she continued reading her screen.

"Is it Molly?" Caleb asked, stepping closer as his brother protested, "But it's Christmas Eve."

Tessa sighed and stuck her phone in the back pocket of her jeans. "Jo's calling in backup." She kissed Jamie quickly as the women gathered their coats and bags. "I'm not sure how late we'll be, so don't forget, you need to pick Julie up from Cheryl and Ricky's by ten."

"I won't forget our daughter on Christmas Eve," Jamie said, rolling his eyes. He lowered his voice, as though they couldn't all hear him. "Don't stay out too late. You promised we could try out your new present tonight."

"Jesus Christ," Ethan swore. "How many times do I have to tell you not to say that shit to my daughter when I'm around?"

Neither Jamie nor Tessa looked terribly contrite despite their mumbled apology. As the women headed towards the door, already speculating about what exactly could require Jo to call in the cavalry on Christmas Eve instead of coming to family dinner, Kyla paused at Caleb's side. "It will be okay." She squeezed his forearm. "Whatever happened, it will all work out. You'll see."

"How do you know?" he asked around the lump in his throat.

She smiled. "Because it's Christmas."

Caleb watched them leave, though he seriously considered going with them. Gavin clapped him on the shoulder, steering him away from the door and back towards the table where Jamie was pouring them all another round of Scotch. "Start at the beginning, big brother."

So he did. He told them about his first day at St. Anthony's High and how Molly had given him a tour of the building, pointing out the coffee maker in the teachers' lounge that liked to randomly shock people and teaching him the trick to unlocking the wonky side door. He told them about chaperoning the senior ski trip together and that night last May when he'd almost kissed her, the time she'd visited him at the church and he thought she might kiss him. He told them about the way she challenged him on the harm done by the Church, how she made him face his role in it. He told them about spiked hot chocolates and sleeping next to her and breaking his vows underneath the Christmas tree—though he kept the specifics to himself. And then he told them about coming home and the panicked look in her eyes when she'd said she needed space, her bombshell about a job offer out of town, her insistence he not change his life for her.

"But she's already changed my life!" he said, pleading with his friends to understand. "She's been changing my life little by little for eighteen months. I could no more keep being a priest now than I could swim across an ocean!"

"He's a sucky swimmer," Gavin said, leaning closer to Jamie as though he were sharing a secret.

Caleb ignored him. "I resigned. Tonight was my last Mass."

"If Molly were to tell you tomorrow that she didn't want to be with you, would you regret resigning?" Jamie asked.

"No." He sliced his hand through the air. "I needed to walk away. I've needed to for a while. Molly helped me see that, but I didn't make this decision overnight. It's something I've been thinking about for a long time."

"Then that's it. You just need to help her understand," Ethan said.

"If it was that simple, I would be out doing it and not here talking with you four," Caleb said.

"It *is* that simple," Baz replied, setting down his empty Scotch glass. "You've been in love with her for over a year. Tell her that."

"He can't just *tell* her," Gavin protested. "He has to *show* her."

"Gav's right," Jamie said. "That first year, Tessa would get skittish sometimes, and I'd—"

"Careful," Ethan warned, eyeing his friend-turned-son-in-law.

"I'd find a way to show her how much she meant to me," Jamie finished, rolling his eyes at Ethan. "Little things to let her know I was paying attention and I wasn't going anywhere."

Caleb considered his friends' advice. If he could show Molly this wasn't a spur of the moment decision for him, that he'd been dreaming of a life with her—and without the priesthood—for over a year, then he could help her see she didn't need to give him space, not for his sake anyway. Molly was a caregiver, willing to fight for anyone's happiness but her own. It was high time someone showed her that *her* happiness was worth fighting for—and if she wouldn't do it herself, he'd do it for her.

And if her happiness means a new job in Boston?

Then he'd pack his bags and move to Boston.

"Do you know how to bake?" he asked Jamie.

"I am a professional chef," Jamie replied with mock offense.

"Is that a yes?" Baz challenged.

"I mean, I don't know exactly, but I do have access to my wife's recipes," Jamie said. "Why are we baking?"

"I have an idea, but if I'm going to pull it off, I'll need your help." Caleb looked around the table at the friends who were so much more like family, each one of them ready to spend their Christmas Eve helping him fight for the woman he loved. "Gav, can you go to Mom's and see if she has any templates left in the recipe drawer?"

"On it," Gavin said, saluting before he grabbed his coat and practically sprinted from the restaurant.

"Ethan, can you see if there's any place open in town selling candy?" Caleb asked.

Ethan snorted. "No need. I have a box at home full of the good stuff."

Baz smirked. "You have a quest for me too?"

"Nope. The three of us are about to bake up a grand gesture," Caleb said, indicating himself, Baz, and Jamie.

"Better not get any flour on my suit," Baz said.

Jamie pushed back from the table, leading the way into his kitchen. "Calm down. I'll let you borrow an apron."

Chapter Nineteen

December 25th

T he wrong woman opened the window.

"What the fuck?" Jo stuck her head out the window of the second-floor apartment she shared with Molly,. She scanned the street below, her eyes finally landing on Caleb where he stood guiltily holding a handful of pebbles, his mouth hanging open. "Well, if it isn't Father West," she said, leaning her forearms on the windowsill. "Why are you throwing rocks at my window, Father West?"

"I was trying to hit Molly's window," he said with a frown, dropping the few pebbles left in his palm.

"Molly's the next window over." Jo tilted her head in that direction. "But don't bother. She isn't there."

Caleb's stomach dropped. "What do you mean? Where is she?"

Jo grinned. Caleb had come to fear that grin, as any sane man would. Nothing good came from Jo Baker grinning like that.

"She had some urgent business over at the school," Jo said. "She wanted to be sure her resignation letter didn't get lost in No-Balls Bruce's spam filter. I told her to wait until after Christmas, but you know Molly, once she's made up her mind about something..."

Caleb stumbled back a step, his shoes sliding in the early morning frost. "What are you talking about?"

Jo pretended to examine her fingernails. "Turns out you're not the only one who can quit their job."

The blood drained from his face, his mouth opening and closing uselessly.

Jo rolled her eyes as though he were the most slow-witted person she'd ever spoken to. "Come on, Father, did you really think she was going to keep working there? Actually, I'm mad at you," she said, jabbing an accusatory finger in his direction. "You've just cost me the best roommate I've ever had."

Everything in him went cold. "What are you talking about? Where is she going?"

Jo shrugged.

He dug into his pocket for his cell phone. The endless ringing on the other end scraped at his nerves. Why wasn't she answering her phone? When it went to voicemail—again—he shoved it back into his coat pocket.

"I need to talk to her," he pleaded with the woman in the window.

"Of course you do," she said, grinning. Somewhere behind her, there was a bang, and Jo turned over her shoulder. "Looks like it's your lucky day. She just got home."

By the time Caleb rounded the building to the front entrance and climbed the two flights of stairs to the door of Molly and Jo's apartment, the gingerbread house his friends had helped him make balanced precariously on an oversized sheet pan, Jo was waiting for him. The door to the apartment was open, but she blocked it with her slight body, leaning one hip against the door frame. She watched him, smirking, as she buttoned her peacoat and tugged on a knitted hat.

"Molly! You've got company!" she shouted before pushing off from the door frame and moving down the hall. "Merry Christmas, Father West."

He stepped just inside the apartment. "Molly?"

He was struck by the sudden realization he'd never been in Molly's apartment before, but his eyes were immediately drawn to the little touches he knew were hers—the poster of Shakespearean insults hanging on the wall over the couch, the perfectly arranged throw pillows, the open bag of gummy bears on the coffee table.

"Caleb? Is that you?" Her voice came from down the hall a moment before she appeared in the living room. She was beautiful. Hair piled on top of her head in a messy bun, bags under her eyes like she'd been up all night, and she'd still never been more beautiful because she was *there*. "What are you doing here?"

He started towards her, then realized he was carrying the gingerbread house and set it down on the coffee table. Her eyes moved between him and the confection, confusion furrowing her brows. "I've been calling you since last night. You didn't answer your phone."

"I dropped it in the sink yesterday. It hasn't turned on since," she said slowly. "Are you alright?"

"No, I'm not alright. Jo said you quit your job." He clenched his hands at his side, wishing he could take her into his arms, but just the night before she'd asked for space and he'd already shown up at her apartment uninvited in the early hours of Christmas Day—so much for space.

"I couldn't exactly keep working there," she said.

"She said you're leaving." The thought tore at his heart, an open wound in his chest he had no hope of closing.

Her eyes went wide. "What? I'm—"

"I know you're scared, Mol. I'm scared too. I'm fucking terrified." His long strides ate up the distance between them. Space be damned, he needed to touch her. Her hands fit so well in his, their fingers intertwined. "I know you think it's too fast. I know you're afraid I'm going to change my mind, but I'm not. I promise you. Don't run away from me, please." He leaned his forehead against hers, breathing in the spicy, citrus scent of her.

"Caleb, I—"

"Wait, don't say anything. Not yet. I need to show you something." He led her towards the coffee table. "I made this for you."

Of all the Christmas gifts Molly had ever received, she never expected a structurally unsound gingerbread house to be the best.

The precarious structure wobbled on the sheet pan as Caleb nudged it closer to the couch. He urged her to sit, before shrugging out of his coat and sitting beside her. She drank in the sight of him, all six-plus-feet of the best man she'd ever known, worry clouding his eyes, his hair standing up in all directions, and his throat... her eyes lingered on the place at the base of his throat where his clerical collar usually sat. The place where, today, the top button was undone, freed from the white piece of plastic that had mocked her for so long.

"You said you didn't want us to make a hasty decision. That you thought I'd regret it because I hadn't given it enough thought." He gestured to the lopsided gingerbread house. "This wasn't a spur of the moment decision, Molly. I've been falling in love with you for over a year, and I'll prove it to you."

"With pastry?"

A flash of a smile crept through the anxiety tugging his lips into a frown. He pointed to a cluster of yellow gumdrops on the candy house roof arranged in the crude shape of a flower. "Last year, when I moved back, that first game night at Ethan's house, you were wearing a dress covered in sunflowers." Her breath caught in her chest. "You looked like summer and I thought I'd never seen someone so beautiful. The next day, I went to the florist and bought sunflowers for my kitchen. I've done it every Saturday since.

"And this—" He pointed to a little pile of hardened icing at the edge of the sheet pan where a gingerbread man stood on sour gummy candy skis with pretzel rod poles. "—this is when we chaperoned the senior ski trip and we stayed up all night talking. Do you know, I'd never stayed up all night before? The morning we got back, I told my confessor I was thinking about leaving the priesthood."

"You—what?" she breathed.

But Caleb didn't answer her. He just continued, pointing out the window carved into the side of the house and filled with melted hard candy in yellow and red and green. "This is for the first time you yelled at me." She laughed, a broken sound colored by the tears gathering behind her eyes. "It was in the chapel at school. You'd just found out sex ed was part of the religion curriculum and you were furious. You were also right."

"Bruce was so mad when you overruled him and made it part of the phys ed curriculum instead."

"Coach Eagles was pretty mad too," he admitted with a chuckle. "But you didn't care that some of your colleagues might not be thrilled. You knew it was wrong, and you pushed me to do something about it. You shouldn't have had to. I should have taken care of it without you needing to point it out. But the point is, you made me better. You *make* me better.

"Last night, I instituted a policy to form a disciplinary committee with student, parent, and faculty representation. No student can be suspended without the approval of the committee, and any student who feels they are being unfairly punished can appeal to the committee. The Superintendent of the Diocese has agreed to oversee the committee's formation and ensure it functions as intended, even though he wasn't too thrilled to get my phone call in the middle of his Christmas Eve dinner."

Her throat constricted with unshed tears. "Caleb, that's amazing. You did it," she said, her voice breaking, as those tears began sliding down her cheeks. "You found a way to work inside the system."

He wiped a tear away with his thumb, his big hand cupping her face and his fingertips lingering at the nape of her neck. "It was my last official act as the pastor of St. Anthony's. I submitted my resignation just after Mass."

She didn't have words for the ways Caleb twisted her up inside, like he was weaving together her veins and nerves in new patterns, rewriting her genetic code and making her into something entirely new. Something entirely his.

And now he was entirely hers as well.

His eyes crinkled at the corners as he studied her, as though he could read her mind and could see the overwhelming sense of rightness filling her up at belonging to him and having him belong to her in return. She half suspected she'd float away from the joy of it if he weren't grounding her with his palm on her cheek.

Before she could say any of that, though, he spun the sheet pan around to reveal a collection of Easter bunny marshmallow peeps wearing gumdrop Santa hats arranged in a semi-circle around a mini chocolate Santa laying in a bed of frosted shredded wheat. On the wall of the house behind them was the image of Santa Mouse painted in royal icing, and beside the chocolate Santa, a tiny wedge of Swiss cheese.

"The last two days with you have been the best days of my life. I can't go back to how things were before, and I don't want to," he said.

She couldn't help the laugh bubbling up inside her, like champagne bursting from a newly opened bottle. He'd unlocked her in ways she didn't know she'd been closed before. "You made me a marshmallow peep nativity scene."

His smile was radiant, lighting up his whole face. "I did."

She swallowed back a sob, ducking her head as the tears fell faster, but he wouldn't let her escape his searching gaze. He caught her chin with his thumb and forefinger, lifting her eyes to his. "I didn't decide to change my life overnight, but you *have* changed my life, Molly Proulx. I could never regret that."

She gripped his forearm and closed her eyes, letting it sink in. He was here, choosing her, and it was still scary—maybe love always was—but the thought of being without him, even for another day, was even scarier.

He brushed his lips over her temple. "Please, love. Say something."

"I made you something too."

Relief danced in his eyes as he stroked her jaw with his thumb. "Yeah?"

"Come see."

She tugged him to his feet and led him into the small kitchen where the remnants of her whirlwind girls' night cluttered the counters. But Caleb didn't seem to notice the mess of dirty dishes and half-drunk bottles of wine on the counter—he was too focused on the project on the dining room table.

"It's not finished yet," Molly explained. "Sabrina said it could take up to a week for the clay to dry properly and then I have to glaze everything, and until they finish drying they're too fragile to move. But I didn't want to wait a week for you to see it, so I went out this morning to borrow Kyla's camera. I was going to bring you a picture after Mass this morning." His throat worked as he swallowed repeatedly, his eyes locked on the dining room table, but he hadn't said anything. "Of course, now I know you wouldn't have been at Mass anyway."

"You made me a nativity scene?" he asked, cutting off her rambling.

Her stomach fluttered and she pointed at each of the ill-formed, half-dried clay sculptures in turn. "Mary and Joseph are Santa and Mrs. Claus. There are reindeer mixed in with the cows. It's a little hard to tell because only Sabrina really knows how to sculpt and Tessa said it wasn't all that different from modeling chocolate, but Jo, Kyla, and I struggled. Anyway, that is supposed to be baby Jesus wearing a Santa hat."

"Are those elves wearing angel wings?"

She nodded. "They're the wisemen. I wanted to show you, we can make it work. I know I won't always understand, but your faith is one of the things I love about you, Caleb. We can find a way to blend the secular and the sacred. At least, I'd really like to try."

He tore his eyes away from the chaotic nativity scene, his brow furrowed. "But you quit your job."

"I'm in love with a priest. How could I keep working for the Church that says I shouldn't love you?"

He cupped her jaw, his eyes softening. "You love your job."

"I love my students. That doesn't change, even if I'm not their teacher anymore. I'll find a new job. One where I don't spend all day trying to protect my students from rules I don't agree with."

"Jo said you're leaving..."

"Jo is convinced she needs to find a new roommate because I'm going to want to live with you instead." She smiled. "She's not wrong."

His eyes darted between hers. "What about Boston?"

She shook her head. "I turned them down. I am officially unemployed." Her smile matched his own.

"That makes two of us."

He pulled her into his arms, holding her close and burying his nose in her hair. She turned her face into his neck, breathing in the pine and sandalwood scent of his skin. It smelled like Christmas miracles. Like home.

"I don't want space, Caleb," she said, fisting her hands in the back of his shirt. "I want you. I was scared. I'm sorry."

He breathed in deeply, exhaled slowly, the rise and fall of his ribs against her chest a comfort. "Last night, when you didn't come to Mass—"

"I'm sorry."

"Shh. There's nothing to forgive. When you didn't come, I found myself praying, harder than I've prayed in years. And do you know what happened?" He pulled away to look at her and she shook her head, searching his eyes. "I heard my answer, clear as day. Whether it was God, or my dad, or just my own heart—it doesn't matter. I heard it."

"What did it say?"

"'Believe.'" He stared into her eyes, the corners crinkling as a smile overtook his face. "I believe in you and me, Molly, the way I believe there is more to this life than I can see. Because I can feel it. Because something that makes me feel this way can't be wrong. I love you."

"I love you."

He kissed her deeply, slowly, because they had no need to rush, no need to hide. Joy overtook her as she sank into his kiss and gave herself over to the magic of loving—and being loved—by him.

"Even if I think *Die Hard* is a Christmas movie?" he teased, skating the tip of his nose against hers.

"Even then, you philistine."

He chuckled, the sound deep and warm, like coming home or curling up in front of the fire. Like her very own Christmas miracle.

"Merry Christmas, Caleb."

He grinned against her lips. "Merry Christmas, Molly."

Epilogue

The following December

"**Y**ou're not supposed to be here." Gavin frowned at Molly as she hiked up her wedding dress and climbed the stone steps to St. Anthony's. He crossed his arms in front of himself as though he were warding off a demon and shook his head. "Uh uh. You're not supposed to see each other before the wedding. It's bad luck."

Molly rolled her eyes and dropped the hem of her dress, the layers of chiffon and lace falling around her turquoise heels. "Caleb doesn't believe in luck."

Gavin hesitated, clearly trying to come up with his next objection. Kyla appeared at the base of the steps, cradling her very pregnant belly with one hand and holding her burgundy dress up with the other so the fabric wouldn't drag on the sidewalk. "Gavin, just let her in. You remember how we were before our wedding."

Her brother-in-law-to-be blushed, the tips of his ears going red, and Molly knew she'd won. "Thanks, Ky!" she called over her shoulder as Gavin grumbled a half-hearted protest, even though he was already descending the steps to meet his wife.

The front door of St. Anthony's creaked as Molly entered the church. The lingering scent of frankincense and myrrh mingled with the Christmas greenery as she entered the sanctuary along, a welcome wave of heat hitting her as she crossed the threshold. Her wedding dress wasn't exactly meant for extended periods of time outdoors in a Rhode Island winter, especially not on a day like today where the air smelled like snow.

It had been almost a year since she'd last been inside a Catholic church, but every so often Caleb would come to a service or just sit in the empty sanctuary and pray. From a pew in the front row, Caleb turned at the sound of Molly's footsteps echoing in the otherwise empty space. He grinned, then put a hand over his eyes. "Isn't it bad luck to see the bride before the wedding?"

"You sound like your brother."

He chuckled and dropped his hand. His eyes slowly swept over her, from the short, simple veil pinned into her hair to the deep V neck between her breasts, the dip at her waist before the lace hugged her hips, to the tip of her turquoise shoes peeking out under the hem, and back up again. His eyes sparkled, liquid and deep in a way that raised goosebumps along her arms.

"You look..." He blew out a breath and took another long look.

She spun around, showing him the low cut back, the way the dress was molded to the curve of her backside. "You like it?"

"I love it. I can't believe I get to marry you."

How did he still manage to make her heart flutter even after all this time? When he got up early to make her coffee before she headed to work at Aster Bay High, or when he stopped on his way home from work at the Women's Resource Center to pick up her favorite bananas foster cupcakes from Tessa's bakery—every day in a thousand little ways, from doing the dishes without being asked to surprising her in the shower with a good morning orgasm, he set her heart racing.

"Sit with me?" He held out his hand to her, helping her arrange the layers of fabric as she joined him on the pew, their clasped hands resting in her lap.

"I thought you would have left for the vineyard by now," she said. The rest of the bridal party had already assembled at Nuthatch, the vineyard Ethan and Hannah owned on the other side of town, and it wouldn't be long before the guests started arriving.

Worry pulled at the corners of his mouth. "Am I late?"

"No. We have time."

They sat in comfortable silence for a moment, Caleb's eyes trained on the stained glass above the altar and Molly focused on him. She could see the thoughts swirling behind his eyes, the silent prayers he was reciting. At last, he smiled and lifted her hand to his lips, pressing a kiss in the center of her palm.

"Do you know what I prayed for?" he asked. She shook her head. "I prayed that we will always be this in love. When I got here, the words wouldn't come, and I realized it's because I don't need to pray for us to be happy. I already know we will be." She squeezed his hand, her stomach doing that swooping thing it so often did when Caleb talked like this, his quiet confidence in their love something she wasn't sure she'd ever get used to. "So instead I offered up a prayer of gratitude, for you, for us, for the life we have together. So many things to be thankful for. I guess I lost track of time."

"Can I add one more thing to the list?"

He grinned and nodded, closing his eyes in prayer and waiting for her to speak. Molly brought his hand to her stomach, holding it flat against the curve of her belly. "Thank you," she murmured.

His eyes flew open, a question poised in them as his gaze darted between her face and her belly. "Are you..."

She bit her lip to hold back her answering smile. "The doctor just called a little while ago. I didn't want to wait to tell you—"

He pressed his lips to hers, cutting off her words. "You're pregnant?" he asked between frantic kisses, his free hand cupping her face. "We're having a baby?"

"Looks like you're going to be a father again after all, Father West," she teased.

He laughed and pulled her into his lap, his kisses slowing, deepening, until she could hardly catch her breath. She shifted in his lap, tugging her skirt up around her hips to allow her to straddle him in the pew. He slid his hands up her thighs, caressing her with a reverence she'd never take for granted. His smile turned wicked as his hands climbed higher then skated away again, up and down in a slow slide that set her nerve endings on fire.

"What are you thinking, angel?" he asked, his voice low and teasing.

She glanced around the empty church and rocked her hips against his growing erection. He groaned at the friction, digging his fingertips into her thighs. "Did you know, for some women, pregnancy increases their sex drive?"

"You don't say." He pulled her hips down in a slow wave, over and over, his own hips lifting slightly to grind against her through their clothing. "One more thing to be thankful for."

He wrapped an arm around her lower back and crushed his mouth to hers as he tumbled them to the floor, the cool marble of the dais a shock against her overheated skin. He pillowed her head on his arm as he dug under her skirt with his other hand. She'd had fantasies like this, finding Caleb alone in the church and giving in to the sexual tension between them, needing each other so badly they couldn't wait for a more appropriate setting, but she'd thought she'd missed her chance to make the fantasy a reality when he'd left the priesthood. Knowing he'd left for her, that they would be husband and wife in a matter of hours, did nothing to dull the adrenaline rush of the forbidden when his fingers slid inside her panties.

"So ready for me already," he marveled. He lightly circled her clit, but even that small amount of pressure here, laid out on the dais in the middle of the church, sent shockwaves through her. "So sensitive. Can I make you come, love? Here, before God, in your pretty wedding dress, with my baby in your belly?" Another circle, a sharp gasp spilling from her lips. "Say yes, angel."

"Yes," she panted.

His smile was predatory and stunning, eyes crinkling at the corners and the light filtering through the stained-glass window making the silver in his hair sparkle. He lifted her skirt and positioned his shoulders between her legs, hooking his arms around her thighs and opening her up to him. He dragged his nose along the crease at the top of her leg, breathing her in, then he hooked her panties with his index finger and pulled them to the side. The cool air of the church against her heated skin sent a shiver through her and her hips drove up, seeking his touch.

He didn't make her wait. He tongue lapped at her in slow, steady strokes, the tip of his tongue swirling beneath the hood of her clit until she was swollen and ripe, begging for release. "I'll make an offering of your pleasure," he murmured. "With my body, I worship you."

She dug a hand into his hair, holding his mouth against her. "Isn't that the wrong religion?" she asked breathlessly.

"It's all the same God," he said.

When he sucked her clit between his lips, she lost the power of speech, given over to the mindless need to come, her hips chasing the pleasure his mouth offered. Her cries echoed in the empty church as she came, Caleb holding her tight against him as he licked her through her orgasm. At last it subsided, and he sat back on his heels, tearing at his belt with one hand as he wiped her release from his lips with the other.

The first thrust always caught her off guard. The burn and stretch of his thick cock as it breached her opening punched the air from her lungs before the bite of pain melted into a pleasure so deep it had woven itself into the fabric of her body. He steadied himself on his forearms above her as he made love to her, slow and deep. Her body softened for him, opening to him by degrees, as it always did, until he was fully seated inside her. The fullness was overwhelming, like she was being pulled apart at the same time she was being made whole.

"Caleb," she gasped, clawing at his back as she urged him to move faster.

"I know, love." He shifted his weight onto one arm, using his free hand to hike her leg over his hip, the adjustment allowing him to move deeper. "You are a revelation. The answer to all my prayers. I promise to always love you, to be your partner in all things."

Tears welled in her eyes as she recognized pieces of the wedding vows they'd written to recite to each other, her heart cracking open as he drove her towards her next climax. A tear rolled down the side of her face and he pressed his lips to the spot, kissing it away.

"I promise to laugh with you, to make my life with you, and never to run from you," he continued as the pad of his finger found her clit, strumming against the over sensitive bud. He thrust faster, his breathing labored. "I promise to make you come as often as you'll let me, to care for your pleasure more than my own, to make love to you all the days of my life."

Her laugh was breathless. "That isn't in the vows."

"It's in the secret vows," he said, nipping at her earlobe. "The ones just for us."

She came with his name on her lips, wave after wave of pleasure drawn from deep within her until she thought it might never stop. And maybe it wouldn't. Maybe this is what it felt like to love with every part of herself, to trust with every part of herself.

As her orgasm crested and Caleb gave himself over to his own climax, filling her, a bone deep joy and calm swept over her. She lifted her eyes to the stained glass above the altar and gave thanks for this man, for this life, for the future they'd share. There, as close as two people could be, before God, he whispered his love for her into her skin, like a vow. Like a prayer.

The End

Also by Cara Dion

Aster Bay series:

Whisking It All
Just For Show
First Comes Marriage
Claim to Fame
Holly Jolly Heresy

Love Song series:

Irreplaceable
Indiscreet
Undeniable

**Visit my website to learn more
and download free bonus content:**

About the Author

Cara Dion writes spicy contemporary romance with swoony heroes. Her debut series, *Love Song*, was released in 2023.

Voted "most likely to write the great American novel" by her middle school classmates, she has been writing for as long as she can remember. Cara has a master's degree in English Literature and has been a high school English teacher, professional musician, and nonprofit administrator.

Cara has always had an overactive imagination and spent much of her teenage years watching 80s and 90s romcoms with her aunt. She read her first romance when a friend snuck one of their mother's Harlequins into their Catholic high school and passed it around like contraband, but Cara didn't return to romancelandia until the pandemic. When she's not reading or writing romance, she loves cooking, Broadway musicals, and all things Disney.

She lives in a small town in New England with her husband, son, and very demanding cat.

Visit her website at www.caradion.com to learn more about Cara's books. Follow Cara on Instagram at caradion.author and contact her at cara@caradion.com.